THE VANDEMARK MUMMY

Cynthia Voigt

FAWCETT JUNIPER • NEW YORK

RLI: $\dfrac{\text{VL 5 \& up}}{\text{IL 6 \& up}}$

A Fawcett Juniper Book
Published by Ballantine Boos
Copyright © 1991 by Cynthia Voigt

Library of Congress Catalog Card Number: 91-7311

ISBN 0-449-70417-3

This edition published by arrangement with Atheneum Publishers, an imprint of Macmillan Publishing Company.

Manufactured in the United States of America

First Ballantine Books Edition: October 1992

*For all of us who have, and are,
brothers and sisters*

❖ 1 ❖

Phineas Hall rode full speed along the brick sidewalk and then stopped dead at his sister's feet. He let the momentum of braking lift the rear wheel up while he swung it behind him; at the same time, in a parallel motion, he swung his right leg up and over, to dismount.

Althea clapped her hands sarcastically, *clap, clap, clap*.

Phineas wheeled the bike over to the rack in front of the three-story brick library. His was the only bike in the rack. The campus was pretty empty during the week before the college opened for summer classes. He didn't bother putting the lock on. He hadn't locked his bike once since they had arrived in Maine, five days ago. Althea had given up nagging him about it.

He went to sit beside her on the bottom step. She already had her nose back in her book, but she lifted it out again. "You're on time."

He didn't know why she bothered saying that. "I always am," he said, and didn't know why he bothered.

"You don't even wear a watch."

"Why should I? I don't need one. I just *know*—like ESP," he said. "Woo-oo-ooo," he made Twilight Zone sounds, and waggled his fingers at her.

"Come off it, Phineas. You looked at one of the outdoor clocks—or asked somebody."

"Come off it, Althea," he mimicked her prissy tone.

1

He was irritating her and he didn't mind, even though she was his only company until school started in the fall, and it was only the end of June. She sighed an irritated sigh and got back to her book.

His father said Phineas should wait until Althea finished growing up before he wrote the final page on her, but that was because like any grown-up, his father's idea of heaven was sitting around talking. Worse, his father wanted to sit around talking about what somebody meant who said it three thousand years ago, and wasn't around to be asked what he'd meant. After three thousand years, who cared?

Althea cared, that's who, and his father. "Where's Dad?" Phineas asked.

"Be along in a minute." She didn't look up from the page. Phineas knew what Althea thought of him. She thought he was a dumb jock, immature, and a wiseass. She liked him all right, she just didn't think much of him.

And that just showed how much she knew. Phineas was no jock. He liked sports, but you had to be a lot better than Phineas was to be counted a jock. Phineas was enthusiastic and a good athlete: That was all he was. Like most people, he wasn't a star at anything. It didn't do any good to get bent out of shape about that, did it? So he didn't. Besides, what was so wrong with being ordinary, an ordinary twelve-year-old kid? Nothing, that was what.

"What's that you're reading?" he asked.

"History." She turned a page. "Ancient Greece." She read on. Phineas thought about needling her a little—he knew some ways—but he heard the big wooden library doors swing open, and turned his head to see his father trying to shove through them with an armload of books. Althea ran up the steps to get the door.

2

Phineas watched the two of them come down the steps. Althea had an armful of books and his father had an armful. You could tell just by looking at them that they were related. Two square sturdy bodies, except Althea was shorter, two heads of frizzy red hair, except Dad's was thinning at the top and Althea's was in short ponytails, two people dressed basically alike in the sweatshirt-jeans-and-sneakers style, if you could call that style. Phineas grinned. The only real difference was the lines on his father's face, mostly laugh lines around the eyes and mouth. Lines made a difference, and so did Althea's heavy eyebrows, so dark and thick they looked like they'd been drawn on her face with india ink.

Phineas stood up to get going, but a voice called out. "Just one minute, *Mister* Hall." It was a woman's voice but deep for a woman, almost like a man's. All three of the Halls turned to look at the woman who stood at the top of the steps.

She made them wait while she took a big ring of keys out of her purse, and locked the door. She was a tall, thin woman, in a brown seersucker suit; a narrow woman with no hips to fill out her skirt, and no shoulders to speak of. Her hair was pale, maybe brown, maybe gray. Her face, when she turned around to look at where they were waiting, was long, thin, and pale.

She came down the steps, her purse clutched in front of her. "If you think, *Mister* Hall," she said, looming over Phineas's father.

Or started to say, because Phineas's father interrupted. "I don't believe you've met my family, Lucille. My daughter Althea, and my son Phineas."

She barely looked at them. She was busy being angry.

"Kids, this is Mrs. Batchelor, the college librarian."

"Hello," Althea said, and stuck out her hand.

3

Mrs. Batchelor didn't want to take it, but she had to. Phineas held out his hand. "How do you do."

She shook his hand too, but before she even let it out of her fingers she had turned back to their father.

"If you think I'm going to take this lying down," she said, looming over him.

"Take what?" Mr. Hall asked.

"A library," she announced, "is for books. The purpose of a library, and it is a great purpose, is to contain books, and the knowledge books hold. A library is not synonymous with—and must not be turned into—a shop window." The woman practically spat the last two words out of her mouth, as if they were some seriously nasty bug that had flown into it. She waited about one second in case anyone wanted to say something, then went on, drawing herself up tall. "I wouldn't be much of a librarian if I allowed anything, or anybody, to degrade a library that was in my care. Now would I." It was not a question.

"I'm sorry, Lucille," Mr. Hall said. "I don't have any idea what you're talking about. Is there a problem I can help with?"

She puffed and snorted. "Don't expect me to be pacified by your boyish charm. The final word has not been spoken. I am not as helpless as I might seem to you. No, don't even try to protest—that's all I'm prepared to say right now," she said; and, as good as her word, she turned her back on all three of them and marched off.

"What was that about?" Althea asked.

"I have no idea," Mr. Hall said. "Not the faintest glimmer."

"She's scary," Althea said.

"Not scary," Phineas said, "weird. Seriously weird."

Mr. Hall changed the subject. "Anybody else want a bite?"

"Me," Phineas said.

"Do we walk or take our bikes?" Mr. Hall asked.

"Bikes," Phineas said.

"Walk," Althea decided.

"Ice cream?" Phineas asked.

"Pastries," Althea said.

"We'll walk into town and get ice cream," their father told them.

They sat in a booth, with Phineas getting a side to himself. Since they'd arrived in Maine, and started settling in, they'd gone downtown at about the same time each day for what his father called a bite. The bite kept them going until they went into town for pizza, at about eight. Phineas guessed that when they finished unpacking, his father would get around to filling the icebox with more than milk and juice and boxes of cereal.

"Hot fudge, two scoops of vanilla, and nothing else, please," Phineas ordered, as usual.

"You want a glass of water with that?" the girl asked, sort of twinkling her eyes at him.

"Yeah, thanks." He wouldn't look at her, although he could feel her twinkling away above him. He studied his menu, as if he cared about what was on it. The trouble with looking older than you were was that girls decided you were cute enough to flirt with, girls who if they knew you were twelve wouldn't look twice at you. But he couldn't just blurt out, "I'm only twelve, leave me alone." That would be seriously dumb. He kept his eyes on the menu and waited for her to go away.

Althea asked for a piece of blueberry pie with chocolate ice cream. "And a glass of water, please."

Mr. Hall smiled up at the waitress. "Water for me too, and two scoops of pistachio, with marshmallow sauce on it, I think, and whipped cream, and some wet nuts, and a maraschino cherry." Phineas lowered the menu.

"How was—?" Mr. Hall tried to ask.

"You shouldn't, Dad," Althea interrupted.

"I like maraschinos," he said, not needing her to explain shouldn't what.

"Think about what they put in to get them that color."

"No," Mr. Hall said, "I don't think I will, and I don't want to hear any more about it, Althea. I've got enough to worry about. My classes start Monday, I have only half my books unpacked, too many nations are developing nuclear weapons, waste disposal is reaching a crisis . . . I think I'll go ahead and have a maraschino cherry on my sundae."

"That's no way to get problems solved," Althea insisted.

Mr. Hall turned to Phineas. "How was your afternoon?"

"Fine. It was okay. I rode around," he told his father, before his father had to ask him.

"I think we're going to like it here," Mr. Hall said. "It's the air that gets me, because it tastes good. It just—knocks me out, the air does. Gives me energy."

"That's a contradiction in terms," Althea said.

"Who says only women get to be contradictory? What do you think, equality is a one-way street?" Mr. Hall asked. "How are the Greeks?"

"The Greeks are fine, it's their verbs I'm having trouble with," she said. "Where'd you ride, Fin?"

"Just around. There are tennis courts, in the park downtown. Clay courts," he said. They knew he wasn't asking them to give him a game. They were the unathletic members of the family.

"Are you sure you don't want to find a day camp to enroll in?" his father asked.

"I'm too old."

"It's going to be a long summer."

"I'll be okay."

"Maybe," Althea suggested, "you should go hang around those courts, with your racket in your hand, looking pitiful. Or looking eager and aggressive, maybe that would be better."

"Maybe you should go fly a kite," Phineas answered.

"Speaking of kites," Mr. Hall said, before either of them could get started on a quarrel, "there's a park in South Portland where people do fly kites on weekends. Home design kites, and trick kites"—he leaned back, so the waitress could put his sundae down in front of him—"it's supposed to be fun on Sunday afternoons, Howie was telling me."

For a few bites, nobody said anything. Things were pretty desperate if watching people fly kites was something interesting to do. Then, "Who's Howie?" Phineas asked, not that he cared. He cared about enjoying his sundae in peace, if anyone was interested, which they weren't. The trick with hot fudge was to space out the sauce, so you didn't run out of sauce before you ran out of ice cream.

"Howie Unnold. Math. His wife is computers." Mr. Hall spoke between spoonfuls of green ice cream topped with thick white syrup topped with mounded white whipped cream topped with brown nuts. "Sandy. Howie and Sandy Unnold. They've been here three or four years, they've got an older house in the city. They're fixing it up. And three kids. All young, the oldest is

7

eight, I think. Can I give them your name for baby-sitting, Althea?"

"I'll be fine, Dad," Althea said. "You don't have to find things for me to do. I'm doing fine."

He didn't look like he believed her.

"We're not the ones being chased down the library steps by angry women," she pointed out. "What *did* you do to get her so angry?"

"Nothing. Cross my heart. I didn't do anything."

"Maybe she doesn't like short guys with frizzy hair," Phineas suggested.

"She didn't seem to like you any better," his father argued.

"Maybe she doesn't like men," Althea suggested.

"She's married," Mr. Hall argued.

"Maybe she doesn't like her husband," Phineas continued—and didn't need the look Althea shot at him to be sorry.

"Then maybe her husband wanted the job you got," Althea said.

"He can't want my job, he works for the art museum."

"Were you assigned her office?" Phineas asked. "Or her parking place? Did you use her coffee mug?"

"No, no, and no," his father said. "No, it's got to be a mistake of some kind. It makes no sense. She was angry."

"And at you, personally," Althea added.

"When I find out what it was, I'll exercise my famous boyish charm," Mr. Hall said, and they all started laughing. "But I hope it gets cleared up quickly," he said. "This is the first job in fifteen years that I'm not overqualified for, and I plan to enjoy it, and I'd hate to find that I've made an enemy of Lucille Batchelor without even knowing how."

"I dunno," Phineas said, "it might be fun. Exciting. She looked like a piece of spaghetti, didn't she?"

Althea grinned.

"A piece of angry spaghetti," Phineas said.

Both of them were grinning at him now, just waiting.

"A piece of angry, whole wheat, health food spaghetti," he said. He was enjoying himself. They were all three enjoying themselves. They were fine, just the three of them.

✠ 2 ✠

HOME, AT VANDEMARK COLLEGE, WAS ONE OF FIVE little houses that lined up tidily along a gravel roadway. Each house sat on a square of grass. Each square of grass was enclosed by a knee-high picket fence. When Vandemark College was the Vandemark Estate, servants lived in these houses. Now the college used them for faculty housing. Because the Halls' house in Westchester hadn't sold yet, they were in no position to buy a house in Portland. Because Mr. Hall was on a one-year contract, and it might not be renewed, he was glad to rent one of the small gable-roofed houses. Even if the rooms were dark and the furniture massive, the house was a five-minute walk from the center of campus, a ten- or fifteen-minute walk from downtown.

That afternoon when they arrived home, Althea pulled the mail out of the letter box, and they all went into the kitchen. Althea sorted the mail. Phineas didn't pay any attention. He never got letters. He didn't write any. If he moved back to Westchester, they'd pick up where they left off, he figured. If he never moved back, what did they have to say to him, Bobby and Phil, Davy, Jason K. and Jason P. and Jason A., Josh, Gerry, Mark? He didn't have anything to say to them. You couldn't exactly play D&D or tennis in a letter, or go for a skate, or do anything worth doing in a letter.

"Letter for you, Fin," Althea said. "From Mom."

The letter was addressed to Phineas Ciamburri-Hall

10

with a return address from Anne-Marie Ciamburri-Hall in Portland, Oregon. She knew he was going to drop the double-barreled name up here; he'd told her. It was a pain, with people never knowing how to pronounce Ciamburri, and having to spell it out all the time. She was ignoring that, he guessed. He held the letter in his hand, without opening it.

"One for me too, and a thick one for you, Dad," Althea said.

They all three stood looking at their envelopes. "I never got a letter from your mother before," Mr. Hall said. His was a brown manila envelope, addressed to Sam Hall, Vandemark College, Portland, Maine. "It *is* thick," he said. He opened it carefully. "Pictures," he said, and unfolded the piece of paper, to read.

Althea and Phineas read theirs. Nobody sat down. "Hey kiddo," Phineas's mother wrote, "how are things in Vacationland? Things here are rainy and I start work tomorrow." She told him about the apartment, and the swimming pool and tennis courts that came with it, about what movies were playing and where she'd seen kids and what they were doing. It wasn't a very long letter. At the end she said, "I admit it, I almost miss the mess, and the smell of old feet. You wouldn't consider sending me one of your previously owned socks, would you? I could hang it up in the spare bedroom." Phineas grinned. He'd been wondering what he'd say when he wrote her back, because he was going to have to write her back, and he thought it would be pretty funny to really send her a sock. First he'd wear it for a few days, until it got seriously smelly.

"She sounds okay," Althea reported. "Lots of museums and concerts, libraries."

"She gets cable TV with the apartment," Phineas reported.

They looked at their father. He spread the photographs around the table, so they could all look at them. "It looks like a pretty typical apartment complex, don't you think? Not swinging singles."

"How can you tell that from pictures?" Phineas asked.

"The parking lot. I figure swinging singles have smaller, newer cars. There's a nice mix of station wagons here, and big old sedans."

"I don't think Mom will like it," Phineas said. "It looks like a giant motel."

"She likes the job," Althea reminded them.

"The job's why she's there," Mr. Hall reminded them. "A job she couldn't turn down. It's the congressman who worries *me*."

"Really?" Phineas asked.

"Yeah, really. He's much too good-looking, and much too unmarried, and your mother is—a heart-stopper."

Phineas didn't have any idea what to say about that. Luckily, Althea did. She not only looked like their father, she thought like him too. Phineas looked and thought like his mother, mostly.

"Once Mom makes up her mind, nothing can change her," Althea said. "You know that, Dad."

"We all made the decision together," Mr. Hall said.

"You and Phineas and I did." Althea wasn't going to budge. "She'd already made hers, no matter what we did."

"Be fair, Althea. Your mother is the one who earns big money."

"That's the argument she used, and it's not honest," Althea said. "This job here, teaching college, is your chance. It's the first time you asked us to move to your job. Equality doesn't mean that women get to drag their

12

husbands around after them, the way men used to do women, all their working lives. Does it? It means everyone has a chance."

"It was just bad timing," Mr. Hall said. "Your mother isn't any happier about it than we are."

"I didn't say I was unhappy," Althea pointed out.

"No," her father agreed, "you didn't. You just suddenly decided that you couldn't live if you didn't know enough Greek to translate Sappho, and buried your face in books. A psychologist would go to town on that, Althea."

Althea shrugged. Phineas didn't know why they were bringing it all up again, since the decision had been made weeks ago, and there was nothing more to be argued about.

"You and Mom don't have exactly the same set of values, you know," Althea said.

"I know," Mr. Hall agreed.

"If you ask me," Phineas said, "which I notice nobody is, it's pretty dumb to break up over a BMW. It wasn't even our BMW. What does it matter to us if the Tunneys give their kid a BMW for a sixteenth-birthday present?"

"We haven't broken up," his father said.

It turned out, that was what Phineas really wanted to hear. Between the fancy apartment—fireplace in the living room, tennis courts and swimming pool—and the congressman, and not having all the irritation of taking care of them—all the nagging and all the cooking—he wasn't too sure what his mother might do next.

"We're not even legally separated," his father said.

"One of the letters for you looks like it's from a lawyer," Althea said then.

"What do you mean?"

13

"Lawyer-type names, with P.A. after it. Mailed in Portland," she warned her father.

He picked the envelope out. It was large, creamy colored, and didn't have the yellow sticker the post office in Westchester put on to forward mail.

"Maine," Mr. Hall said, "Portland, Maine, see? But why would a lawyer here be writing to me?"

"Looking for business?" Phineas suggested. "Lawyers are allowed to advertise you know."

His father had opened the letter, and was reading four short, typewritten lines, holding in his other hand another envelope, even creamier and more expensive-looking than the first. He opened that one too, and read it without even looking up at his children, who stood watching. When he had finished the second page, he was puzzled but amused.

"The effect preceded the cause," he announced. He didn't expect them to understand. "All is explained," he added, which explained nothing to Phineas. He spread the letter on the table for Phineas and Althea to read.

"To Whom It May Concern," the letter began.

It is my eighty-eighth birthday. That need not concern you, just as who you are does not concern me. That I am eighty-eight does concern me. It is time to begin thinking of my demise. When you read this, that event will have occurred.

I have bequeathed to Vandemark College my Egyptian Collection. Do not get your hopes up, young man, and I hope you are scholar enough to restrain the board of governors in what will inevitably be their shortsighted enthusiasm. The Egyptian Collection contains no treasures. It is, however, of historical

14

interest as well as—I flatter my youthful judgment—having some use to scholarship.

You come into the business because I have decided to establish a curatorial chair for the Collection. I have further decided to award that position to the newest appointee in the Department of Classical Languages. This choice may well be idealistic of me, or willful, but I have my reasons. Experience tells me that a scholar may be more clear-sighted in a field other than his own. It tells me, further, that a Classical linguist will possess qualities the Collection will benefit from—a lack of what the world calls ambition (by which word the world usually speaks of greed), and a patient meticulousness of mind. I can only hope that you have these characteristics.

The bequest includes a gift of money sufficient to build a small wing onto the present library. On no account is this building endowment, or the Egyptian Collection, to become an adjunct of McPhail Hall.

The curatorial salary is presently set at the sum of ten thousand dollars per annum, to be adjusted annually for cost of living. You will more than earn it, in the first years. After that, it will perhaps smack of the sinecure. I don't know what your moral structure is, young man, but one should never scorn a sinecure out of hand. It may even, once the real work is done, enable scholarship. I have always admired scholarship.

The Collection, as you will find, is a hodgepodge. There will be some pleasant surprises for you, or so I like to think. The mummy, which is its centerpiece, has a certain wistful appeal, being from the Roman era. I have neglected the Collection, distracted as I became by other interests. I hope it will find a better home at Vandemark College than the cellars where it has spent its time with me. I hope it will find a better curator in you than it had in me. Should any article of the bequest be unfulfilled, then the Collection will return to the disposal of my son and grandson, as joint executors of the entire estate which I will have left behind me, when I have left this world.

I have, I trust, been quite clear. The president will also have been informed of the bequest, and its conditions. I have, I think, foreseen all contingencies, to the best of human abilities.

Yours from the brink of mortality,
Felix K.C. Vandemark II

"Will I be able to help out?" Althea asked. "Do you notice? He assumes you have to be a man."

Phineas noticed what his sister always thought of first—sexist stuff.

"I don't know if I'm qualified," Mr. Hall said.

And that was what his father always thought of first.

"I don't think this guy cared about qualifications," Phineas pointed out.

"It'll give me something to write your mom about."

"She'll be jealous," Phineas said.

"There's nothing to be jealous of," Mr. Hall said. "It's just something a scholar would enjoy."

"Well I can see why Mrs. Batchelor is angry at you," Phineas said. "Who would want a mummy around permanently? Dirty, probably smelly, it's just an old dead body."

"That's really dumb, Fin," Althea said. "It's a collection, the letter says. That means antiquities."

"Yeah," Phineas agreed. He'd been to the Metropolitan Museum on more class trips than he cared to remember. "Broken jars. Pieces of stone with things

16

carved on them in a language nobody has spoken for hundreds of years. Statues with pieces missing.''

''Why don't you two wait and see what it is, before you start fighting about it?'' Mr. Hall asked.

❈ 3 ❈

THE NEXT TEN DAYS WERE BUSY ONES FOR MR. HALL, who, along with his summer school classes, also had frequent meetings with President Blight to discuss how to store the Egyptian Collection until the Building and Grounds Committee could have the proposed addition designed and built, and frequent meetings with Mrs. Batchelor to discuss her objections to everything President Blight and Mr. Hall had agreed on. Mrs. Batchelor was throwing up roadblocks at every point, Mr. Hall told his children.

If, Mrs. Batchelor said, the collection needed temporary housing, why not in McPhail Hall? If the terms of the will forbade that, then why not in the gym? If the gym was open to the public over the summer, couldn't it be closed? The library cellars were already used for faculty offices, and the Sports Department office, and general storage, why did they have to take even more space for nonlibrary purposes? If they were going to go to the expense of an air control system, why couldn't they put it in the rare book room, where there were irreplaceable books and holographs, acknowledged treasures? If they were going to go ahead and ride roughshod over her opinions, they couldn't expect her to like it, could they? If they said that they agreed with her that a library was the heart of any educational institution, they didn't expect her to believe them, did they? Not if they went ahead and did this.

Mrs. Batchelor was not happy. Mrs. Batchelor was not satisfied that the library cellar was the right place for the collection. Mrs. Batchelor felt demeaned, personally demeaned, by what was going on. Mrs. Batchelor was not going to be sweet-talked; her only concern was for the integrity of the library.

Preparations went on regardless of all the meetings. A room in the library cellar was chosen to hold the collection until the new wing had been built. The library cellars were like an underground city, narrow concrete corridors lined with closed, numbered doors. There were no windows, and only one exit to the outside, a door opening onto the parking lot behind the library. There was only one door leading up into the library from the cellar. It was, Phineas thought, the perfect place for storage, like a rat's maze in a scientific laboratory. For the collection, the largest room, number 015, a room the size of a lecture hall, had been emptied. Dehumidifiers and a self-contained heating system had been set up to maintain the correct temperature and humidity for antiquities. Because all the doors of the library opened to a single key, the door into 015 had been fitted with a new lock, to which only Mr. Hall, Mrs. Batchelor, and Captain Lewis of the College Security Squad had keys.

Mr. Hall had taken charge of these preparations. After about the first hour, he hadn't said anything more about not being qualified for the job. Even when President Blight called up, just after the letter had arrived, Mr. Hall didn't say anything about not being qualified. Phineas and Althea could guess what the president was hinting by their father's side of the conversation. "I understand, sir, but luckily I'm a quick learner, and I did have a couple of classical art courses, so I'm not unfamiliar with the field." He grinned at his children.

"It is a pity, isn't it? Unless the will is ambiguously worded, the old gentleman hasn't given me any choice, and I'll just have to manage as best I can."

The morning the collection was due to arrive, a bright Saturday morning, Mr. Hall looked at Phineas and Althea over breakfast. "The big day. You're coming, aren't you?" They were. "It will be a relief to finish with these interminable arguments with Lucille, so I can concentrate on my classes and the cataloging of whatever the collection turns out to be."

Phineas thought it would be a relief to have something happen, anything. He was getting bored with solitary bike riding and solitary TV watching—seriously bored. At least with the Egyptian Collection, he didn't know exactly what was going to happen.

When the Halls arrived at the big grassy quadrangle of which the library formed one side, there was a small crowd gathered. Mr. Hall turned off to join the reception committee—President Blight and his wife, and standing with them a Westchester woman, as Phineas called the type, looking expensively well groomed and expensively well dressed. "A board member, what do you bet," Mr. Hall told Phineas and Althea. "I ought to introduce myself. I feel underdressed." He went toward the president's group, reluctantly.

Phineas and Althea hung back, looking around them. The sky was turquoise blue, and cloudless. The tall leafy trees that grew on the quadrangle cast cool shadows onto the grass. A few students lay around in the sunny patches, talking and tanning and watching the excitement. During the summer only one classroom building, the gym, and the library stayed open. Only those students who lived nearby could take summer classes. Nobody paid attention to Phineas and Althea.

Mr. Hall was standing sort of with the president's group, but mostly aside, ignored. A person—Phineas couldn't tell what sex it was but the way it kept writing things down in a notebook identified it as a reporter—was talking with President Blight. Phineas moved closer to his sister.

"What's a reporter doing here?"

"I guess it's a big deal for the college."

"But I thought it wasn't much of a collection."

"It has historical interest. Just because something's not worth a whole lot of money doesn't mean it doesn't have any value, Fin. Don't be any more of a Philistine than you can help."

"Even junk is a big deal, as long as it's old junk?"

"Jerk," was all his sister had to say to that.

"Oh yeah?" But he couldn't get interested in the quarrel. "Look," he said. "There she is." Mrs. Batchelor, dressed in her usual seersucker suit, emerged from the big glass doors behind a man who was as tall and weedy as she was. He wore khaki slacks and a turtleneck, and managed to look like someone from Greenwich Village, or maybe Paris, France. He looked like someone who was temporarily stranded in an alien environment, or at least he hoped it was temporary. He led Mrs. Batchelor over to where President Blight was standing. They ignored Phineas's father. The reporter hopped around taking pictures.

Phineas didn't like to see his father being pretty much ignored, so he was glad to notice a man with a thick red-gold beard and bright red-gold hair come up to talk to his father. His father looked glad to see the man.

"Who is that?" Althea asked.

"I'll find out." Phineas went over and hunkered down beside the nearest tanners. These were a boy and girl who lay side by side on their backs, hands clasped,

21

faces to the sun, eyes closed. "Excuse me," Phineas said.

They opened their eyes lazily.

"Do you know who the guy with the beard is?" Phineas pointed.

The boy raised himself onto one elbow. The girl closed her eyes again. "Simard," the boy said. "History. Or Dr. Simard, as he likes his students to call him. The Rugman."

"Rugman?" Phineas wondered.

"You know what a rugman is, don't you, kid?"

Phineas didn't want to admit that he didn't. He thought—rugs lie around and get stepped on. He figured a rugman was a wimp, a wussy. He grinned. "What kind of history does he teach?"

The girl answered. "Ancient history mostly, you know, like Babylonians, Phoenicians, Egyptians, Greeks, and Romans."

"Bo-ring," the boy said, lying back down and closing his eyes. "Most boring lectures I ever heard. And he only does lecture courses."

"He publishes a lot. He's successful," the girl said. "Maybe you're the boring one."

"Ha ha. Who's the guy the Rugman's talking to?"

"My father," Phineas said. "He's going to be the curator of this collection."

"If it ever gets here," the boy muttered.

The girl opened her eyes. "What's your name?"

"Phineas. Phineas Hall."

"Nice to meet you, Phineas Hall. You ought to forget what we said about Dr. Simard. I thought you were a townie, otherwise . . ." She closed her eyes again and let the sun fall over her face.

There was nothing more to say, so Phineas reported back to Althea, who didn't even thank him for doing

22

what she was too chicken to do herself. They waited a while more. The president kept looking at his watch. The expensive lady looked at hers, and talked at Mrs. Blight. She looked pretty cranky.

More time passed, slowly. The students drifted away into the library, or the classroom building. The greeting party on the library steps chatted, and stood around, and looked at their watches.

"Why did they say ten-thirty if they didn't mean it?" Althea grumbled. "Who said ten-thirty?" She was always finding out who was to blame, and blaming them. With perfect timing, the motor of a big truck ground in low gear from behind the library. At the same time, two people walked around the side of the building and up to President Blight. Phineas perked up.

They looked like impossible twins, dressed exactly alike in blue blazers over gray flannels, with striped ties. They looked like Schwarzenegger and DeVito, except the tall twin was much older than the short twin, who looked about Phineas's age—overdressed, if those were really tasseled loafers on his feet, seriously overdressed, but a kid like Phineas.

"Come on," Althea said, interrupting his thoughts. "The truck's out behind."

In the parking lot, a medium-size moving truck was backed up to the cellar door, and four men waited beside it. As Phineas and Althea came around the corner, they saw their father step up to talk with the movers.

"If Dad's in charge—" Phineas said.

"We'd better," Althea agreed. They went to stand just behind their father. The rest of the greeting committee stood back, watching what would happen. The head mover passed Mr. Hall a clipboard, holding a thick wad of papers. "Ah," Mr. Hall said, and looked down

23

at the clipboard in his hand, as if he'd never seen one before in his life.

"I can check the containers off," Phineas offered. They'd moved a couple of times in his life, and he was familiar with the process. "You and Althea can show them where to put the things, and make sure they're handled properly." Phineas and his mother were the efficient ones. When anything needed to be done efficiently they stepped forward to take charge.

"Isn't it nice when you have your children to help you out?" Mrs. Batchelor's voice asked. "Yes, nice," a male voice answered, "to have helpful children when you need help."

Phineas ignored them.

"We don't have any," Mrs. Batchelor said. "No," the male voice which had to be her husband's agreed, "we don't."

Which was lucky for the kids, Phineas thought.

"The blind are leading the blind here," Mrs. Batchelor said.

"Let's go home, I've got better things to do than . . ." he answered.

Phineas carefully didn't look up from his clipboard. If he had, he might have laughed. The two of them were so obvious about what they were up to—it was like "Mr. Rogers' Neighborhood," Phineas thought, like Lady Elaine talking with King Friday the Thirteenth, he thought—and laughed out loud.

By the end of an hour, almost everyone had left. Phineas didn't blame them. There wasn't much to see: First, the movers had to learn how to get to room 015, then the driver maneuvered the truck into the right position, then they set up the ramp. Finally they pulled open the rear doors. Once people had peered inside the truck—just lots of boxes, some coffin-size, some crate-size—they went away. Only the reporter, who up close turned out to be a young woman, the bearded Dr. Simard, and the rich kid and his father remained to watch the first crate carried out of the truck.

The two movers who were carrying it stopped in front of Phineas so that he could check off the sticker number. They protested when he looked at it from all sides to see if the box had any signs of damage. "Kid, this is heavy. Besides, it was all packed up when we got there. Packed sometime just after Noah's Ark landed, if you want my opinion. Anything wrong with the packing has nothing to do with us."

"Just checking," Phineas said, and proceeded to do so. He didn't expect to find anything, no crushed ends or things falling out of holes. These were wooden crates, solidly built. "Do you know where to take them?"

"Yes, sir." The man was making fun of him.

Phineas didn't take offense.

It took another hour to unload the truck. Dr. Simard hung around, trying to look, Phineas thought, like he mattered. Phineas stayed put with his clipboard and pen, methodically checking each box and at the same time eavesdropping on the reporter's attempt to interview the rich man, who turned out to be Felix K. C. Vandemark IV. "So you've never actually seen the collection?" she asked. She had short dark hair, in a chunky cut.

"None of the family has, except my grandfather, of course. There are inventory sheets, which I will turn over to Professor Hall, but one can't tell from an inventory sheet what condition the individual object may be in."

"Can I have a copy of the inventory?"

"You'll have to ask Professor Hall about that. He's the curator."

"So, what was your grandfather doing in Egypt, in . . . nineteen sixteen to nineteen eighteen?"

"The war," Mr. Vandemark answered.

"Huh?" the reporter asked.

"The Great War. The First World War."

"Oh, was that on then?"

Behind him, Phineas heard Althea snort. Mr. Vandemark looked at the reporter as if she were some kind of insect, some kind of unpleasant, unwelcome insect. But his good manners kept him stuffy. "Yes," he said.

"What was he, an officer?"

"He wasn't in any army. I was always told that he was an admirer of Lawrence. I have always assumed he was working with Lawrence."

She chewed on the end of her pen. "You mean Lawrence of Arabia? I saw that movie. Peter O'Toole. Did your grandfather know him?"

"I can't think that's relevant," Mr. Vandemark said. He had a square jaw and unfriendly eyes. Phineas would have stopped asking him questions with those eyes looking at him, but the reporter stood her ground.

"So, was your grandfather an Egypt fan all his life?" the reporter asked. "What would that be, an Egyptologist?"

"He was a collector, to put it most accurately. This is just one of many collections."

"What were the others?"

"China figurines, Roman coins, Duncan Pfyffe furniture, eighteenth-century watercolors. He had quite a library of first editions, from the twenties and thirties, prose, fiction, and poetry, some inscribed. Have I forgotten anything, Casey?"

"Japanese ceremonial robes," the boy contributed.

"Yes, Japanese ceremonial robes," he repeated.

The reporter was writing like crazy. "And all of this

is coming to Vandemark College?'' She sounded impressed.

"Mayan pottery,'' the boy said.

"That's right,'' his father said, "Mayan pottery.''

"And all of this—'' the reporter said.

"Edward Lear memorabilia,'' the boy said.

"I think she has enough,'' his father said.

"And all of this is coming to Vandemark?'' the reporter asked.

The man sighed. "Only the Egyptian Collection has been left to Vandemark. The others are going to other universities.''

"Like where?'' She was so busy writing, she didn't see the expression on his face.

"Harvard. Yale. Stanford.'' He marched the names out.

"Why not Vandemark?'' she wondered.

"My grandfather may have thought that when his father gave the land and buildings to found the college, the family had done enough.'' Clearly, Mr. Vandemark thought his family had done enough, and maybe even more than enough.

"So, is there really a mummy?''

"Yes,'' he said, cautious, and also bored.

"And what about the curse? What's the mummy's curse for this one? Like, is your whole family dead?''

Althea guffawed. The reporter turned around, as if surprised to see them. Luckily, Mr. Hall and Dr. Simard emerged from the library cellar in time to hear this, and see Mr. Vandemark's face.

"Miss—'' Mr. Hall said.

"O'Meara. No Miss, just O'Meara. From the *Post*.''

"And a Vandemark graduate,'' Professor Simard said. Something about what he said, or the way he said it, made her scuff her feet, as if she'd suddenly lost about ten years. "You're doing well for yourself if you're working for the *Post*."

"I guess I am."

"The situation is, O'Meara, I can't give you any information right now," Mr. Hall said. "We haven't uncrated the collection. If you call me in, say a week? I can give you a better idea of what there is, so you can do a story. But—none of this mummy's curse stuff, okay? Nobody takes that kind of thing seriously. If there were such things"—his eyes twinkled—"do you know how many mummies there are? Imagine all of them lying in museums and cursing away."

She let this information sink in. "How many mummies are there?" she asked.

Even Phineas choked on that one.

"Call me next week. I'll have more to tell you then," Mr. Hall said. She had to know that he was giving her a hint.

"And keep up the good work," Dr. Simard said.

He didn't sound sarcastic. He didn't look sarcastic either; there was no hint of mockery on what you could see of his face beyond the beard. Maybe he was sincere, Phineas thought.

❖ 4 ❖

THEIR WORK DONE, THE MOVERS FOLDED UP PACKING quilts, replaced ramps, bolted the van doors shut, accepted their check from Mr. Vandemark, and then climbed into the cab. As the truck pulled out of the parking lot, O'Meara looked around.

Nobody said anything to her.

"So, what happens next?" she finally asked.

"I have a class this afternoon," Mr. Hall answered, "and I expect there are some papers Mr. Vandemark would like me to read and sign before he leaves." Hint, hint, Phineas thought.

"Can I get a picture of the boxes in their room?"

"No, the room is locked."

She pounced. "You're keeping it locked? Do you expect trouble?"

Mr. Vandemark rumbled, impatiently. Dr. Simard stepped in. "Give it up, Miss O'Meara. Why don't you go home now, like a good girl?"

He only made her more stubborn. "What kind of locks, Mr. Hall?"

"Tell you what. We could make an appointment for an interview next week. Would that satisfy you?"

"When next week?"

"Call me Tuesday. Is that fair enough?"

There was more she wanted to ask, but she gave it up. "Okay, thanks," she said, folding her notebook closed, dropping her ballpoint pen into a lumpy cloth purse and jamming the notebook in after it. "I'll call you Tuesday."

They watched her walk away, purse banging against one hip, camera banging against the other. They watched her halt and turn abruptly around again. "Morning," she called. "Tuesday morning. Early."

"How can I be jealous of someone like that?" Althea muttered. Phineas answered her just as quietly.

"You're not, are you? Why should you be?"

"She's thin. She stands up for herself."

"You're not fat."

"Ha," Althea said.

"No, I mean it. Fat people jiggle."

"And I have terrible legs."

"Your legs aren't great, but they're not bad," Phineas said.

"What do you know about it?" she demanded.

"I'm a boy," he pointed out.

"That's just what I mean."

Phineas couldn't figure out what to say. Sometimes, he felt guilty about the way their gene pool had gotten distributed. Althea should have been the one to look like their mother. It didn't matter what guys looked like, not nearly as much as what girls looked like.

For that matter, Phineas should have been the one to get his father's brains. It didn't matter as much if girls were smart, he thought. Then he clamped his hand over his mouth, as if he'd actually said the words out loud. What his mother would say if she could hear him thinking that—imagining it made him grin. She'd have a lot to say. Besides, his mother was smart, really sharp. She just wasn't intelligent in the same way his father was. They were pretty different, in that way as well as in looks, and he guessed he could understand if they didn't live together.

30

"What's wrong with your mouth?" Phineas jammed his hand in his pocket. "Dad wants us," Althea went on. "Coming?"

Mr. Hall stood between Phineas and Althea to introduce them. "My children," he said.

Mr. Vandemark dipped his head at them, so they couldn't say he didn't know they existed, Phineas figured. Up close, Mr. Vandemark looked just like Phineas expected him to, like a prize dog ready for the big show, a prize bulldog because of his heavy jaw, all gleaming with food and grooming. The kid silent at his side looked about the same, only short, and his hair didn't have any gray in it.

"I guess I'm extraneous too," Dr. Simard said. "It was a pleasure to meet you, Mr. Vandemark, and say in person how grateful I am, how much the bequest will add to the college. I appreciate—we appreciate—but you're a busy man. And Sam, you know where to find me if you need me."

"Yes, thanks, although I've got these two to help out."

"I know hieroglyphs, and a fair amount of the history, some demotic Greek—but I imagine you know Greek better than I do. I'd be pleased to be of service. You're a lucky man, Sam. I'd envy you more if you weren't qualified for the job."

"Thanks again," Mr. Hall answered. "A vote of confidence is more than welcome."

Dr. Simard smiled, a flash of teeth in his beard. "Don't let Lucille worry you—I expect she's jealous." He was as big, both tall and broad, and as hairy, as a Viking, but his eyes weren't right for the part. They were mild blue eyes, wimp eyes. "Tell you what I do envy," he said, still smiling. "People with children, families." He waved a hand and strode off.

31

"I assume he has no children," Mr. Vandemark said. "Well, I've got six, and I agree with him. That, however, is entirely beside the point. All that is left me to do is explain the details of the bequest to you, and what your responsibilities to the executors will be. I understand you have one of the former servants' houses? We have our picnic hamper with us."

Althea pulled on Phineas's arm, to pull him away.

"There's plenty for all of us," the boy said, speaking for the first time. "You know the kind of lunch Mrs. Willis packs, Dad, as if we were going to feed the king of England."

"There is no king of England," Mr. Vandemark said. The boy flushed.

The picnic came in two wicker baskets that looked like suitcases and were almost as big. It came with its own dishes, utensils, and glasses. The Halls didn't even have to supply napkins, which was lucky, because Mr. Vandemark didn't look like the kind of man to tolerate a paper napkin. Chicken salad, in a covered bowl, a dozen hard rolls with a stick of unsalted butter, three different cheeses, four kinds of fruit, a chocolate cake cut into pieces, a bottle of wine, and a bottle of Perrier water—the picnic filled the dining room table.

Phineas wanted milk and so did the boy, Casey, which gave Althea a chance at the Perrier. Once all of their plates were filled with food, Mr. Vandemark had a speech to make. "I won't attempt to hide it from you, Mr. Hall. The family will not be unhappy if the college fails to meet the terms of the bequest. The family had hoped that Grandfather would donate his Egyptian Collection to the MFA—the Museum of Fine Arts in Boston. It seems a suitable recipient for such a bequest."

Mr. Vandemark was the kind of man who thinks only

he should ever be talking. Phineas looked curiously at Casey: No surprise, the kid was eating quietly, the kind of kid who thinks he's better off not having anything to say.

"Of course, it didn't come entirely as a surprise. Grandfather was a difficult man—self-indulgent, impulsive, just what you'd expect of the first generation after a self-made man. Most of the time the family could control him but a will is between a man and his lawyer. The family feels very strongly that the MFA should have the collection," he said again.

This family was beginning to sound like the SEC and the IRS with a little IRA mixed in. Phineas was already pretty tired of this family. He looked at Casey. Casey lifted his fork to his mouth, his face as expressionless as if he were deaf.

"How unfortunate for you that your grandfather didn't agree," Mr. Hall said.

Mr. Vandemark nodded his head. "I'm glad you understand. He was a trial to his father, a trial to his sister, and a trial to his own children."

"Ummnnmn," Mr. Hall said, his mouth full.

"The proposed addition to the library is of course little more than an attempt to get even with his sister. Olivia—that's your great-great-aunt, Casey—had been left life tenancy in what is now McPhail House, but she donated it to the college, which irritated Grandfather."

"You mean she gave the president his house?"

Mr. Vandemark looked at Phineas for a few seconds before he answered, making Phineas wish he'd kept his trap shut. Phineas bet he could tell what the man was thinking: Children should be seen but not heard. "She gave her house to the college, and the college houses its president there," Mr. Vandemark said, when he was through waiting to speak. "As well as its alumni offices."

Phineas nodded and tried to look alert, as if this was important information he was glad to have.

"The family can only assume that Grandfather intended to catch up with her. In the kind and value of his gift."

Phineas nodded, as if now it was all clear to him.

"It's my father who is the most upset about this. This was the only chance to place a Vandemark gift in the halls of the MFA."

"I can understand your frustration," Mr. Hall said, distracting Mr. Vandemark's attention.

"It's not the money," Mr. Vandemark said. "Nobody would have minded a building, nobody minds. In fact, we rather expected that."

"Should I apologize?" Mr. Hall asked.

"I don't see what good that would do," Mr. Vandemark said. "No, we have to grin and bear it, even you. Because I'm sure you agree that you don't have the qualifications—"

"Well," Mr. Hall said, his eyes bright, "I'll do my best. If that's not good enough, your problems will be solved."

"Although even this particular building project we have our doubts about. We feel the money would be better used in some forward-looking field. The sciences perhaps. Something with its eye to the future. I can promise you, however, that even if the terms Grandfather set up aren't met, no member of the family would attempt to take the money away from the college."

Mr. Hall didn't say anything.

Mr. Vandemark didn't say anything.

None of the kids said anything.

After a while, Mr. Vandemark spoke again. "You'll

want to see the provenance files, and I have your contract here, financial statements, a copy of the will. . . . Why don't you three go outside and play?" he asked, as if he had just noticed the children at the table.

Althea, Phineas, and Casey sat down in a row on the front steps, with Phineas in the middle. Casey studied his tasseled loafers, for a long time. Althea picked at the soles of her sneakers. Phineas didn't have anything to talk to anybody about. The sky was blue. The leaves rustled. You couldn't hear anything—no voices, no cars, nothing.

Finally Casey asked, "Are you two twins?"

"What?" Phineas asked. "Us?" he laughed.

"Well you look about the same age." Casey brushed his hair back, as if it were allowed to grow long enough to fall over his forehead.

"Identical twins, right?" Phineas turned to grin at his sister.

Casey pulled at the tail of his tie. "Then how old are you?"

"Twelve."

"Althea?"

"Fifteen next month."

"Oh," Casey said. He studied his loafers some more. His nose had an interesting bump about halfway down it. Phineas had enough friends to know that you couldn't judge a kid by his parents. "I'm never good guessing ages," Casey said. "All of my brothers and sisters are a lot older than I am. I'm thirteen," he said, although nobody had asked him. "My next oldest sister is going to graduate from college next year. Princeton. I'm an afterthought. Where's your mother?"

"In Portland," Althea answered, before Phineas could say anything.

"Mine stays in Boston, except for some weekends. We come up to Kennebunk for the summer. We always came up for the summer, even before Bush."

Nobody said anything.

"All right, look," Casey finally said, words bursting out of him. "I'm sorry about what my father's been saying. The trouble is, the family is used to getting its own way. Except for Great-Grandfather, nobody ever crossed the family, and as soon as he got old they moved in, with doctors and nurses, and practically kept him a prisoner, to keep him from doing the things they didn't like. I know it's not your father's fault about the collection. I'm sorry about the way my father talks. Mother says that it's lucky he never had to work for a living, because he's so tactless he'd never have gotten above the bottom rung on any ladder. I said I was sorry."

Althea was as puzzled as Phineas. "We don't mind," Phineas said.

"I have a pretty crappy life," Casey said.

"I'm going to the library." Althea stood up. "I've got work to do." She didn't ask if either one of them wanted to go with her. Phineas might have wanted to go with her, that afternoon.

"What work does she do?" Casey asked.

Phineas decided he might as well talk to the kid. He might as well find out if they had anything in common, since this was the first kid he'd met in Portland. Unless he wanted to be stuck dealing only with adults—and Althea—until school started, which he didn't, which he seriously didn't, he'd better make an effort. "She's studying Greek."

"Why?"

"To learn it."

"No, I mean why."

"To learn it," Phineas repeated, stubbornly. Then he

reminded himself that Casey was just trying to be friendly. "She's got this idea, she wants to read Sappho in the original."

"I guess Sappho's Greek?"

"Ancient Greek, even before Homer. You know Homer?"

"Not to say hello to."

It was a pretty weak joke, but Phineas appreciated the effort.

"Why Sappho?" Casey asked.

"Because she's a woman, and a poet, and my mother always says women never had much of a chance to really accomplish much, in art. My mother's a feminist, and it always used to be she and Althea agreed about everything. See"—he turned to face Casey—"the Portland where my mother is is Oregon. She got a job there, and she took it." End of subject, as far as Phineas was concerned. He got up from the steps.

"Is that what's wrong with your sister?"

Phineas turned around. "Nothing's wrong with Althea. Maybe she's shy, because people who don't know her think she's weird. Actually, she's just brilliant." Phineas didn't know why he felt like he needed to defend Althea. She didn't need defending. "Maybe she is upset," he admitted.

"But you aren't?"

Phineas shrugged.

"Why, did they fight a lot or something like that?"

Phineas drew the line. "What makes you so nosy?"

But Casey refused to take offense. "I thought—maybe we'd be friends, and if we were, I thought, I should know."

"Why should we be friends?" Phineas demanded. He didn't care how rude he sounded.

Casey's face lit up with mischief, which made him

look much more like someone Phineas would like to be friends with. It made him look like his flannels and blazer, tie and tasseled loafers were a costume. The wrong costume, Phineas thought.

"Because I know something you don't. The newspaper reporter was only guessing, but she was guessing right. There *is* a mummy's curse." Casey was lying and Phineas knew it, and Casey knew Phineas knew. Casey was just messing around. "What nobody has told you, or your father, is that when my great-grandfather died he looked—nobody had ever seen anyone look like that before. They wouldn't let me see him, but Mrs. Willis went in, and she told me. He looked as if he'd seen something—and his heart stopped. Because when he saw it, it was so terrible, he died. And his hands . . ." Casey held his own hands out in front of him, fingers outspread.

Phineas was mesmerized, waiting for whatever it was he was going to hear next, which would be worse than anything he'd ever heard or imagined before in his life.

"His hands—both of them—all of the fingers were disjointed. The knuckles pulled out of their sockets. As if he'd been trying to pull back against something, something with incredible force that was pulling him out of bed, to take him—Who knows where? Who knows what? Something so strong it dislocated his fingers, and you know what that means?"

Phineas shook his head. This was terrific.

"It means the thing probably had hands too." Casey waited a beat. "Like a mummy had come up to his room, when he was alone in the middle of the night, and *pulled* his life out of him."

"You're lying."

"Am I?"

Phineas thought for a minute, checking his impres-

38

sion. "Yeah, you are." Casey shrugged, grinned, shrugged again. "Listen," Phineas said, "you want to go climb some trees? Or can you, in those clothes? There are some good trees right over there in the woods. I could show you some good climbing trees."

Casey was already undoing his tie. "I've got plenty more clothes. Aren't you even a little scared of the mummy?"

"Why should I be?" Phineas asked. "It's just a dusty old dead person, isn't it?"

❊ 5 ❊

IT WAS LUCKY FOR PHINEAS THAT THE EGYPTIAN Collection had turned up. It gave him something to write about to his mother, in the letter that accompanied a sock he'd worn for three days before he put it in a plastic bag, put the plastic bag into a thick manila envelope, and put the whole shebang into the mail.

Phineas didn't like writing a letter to his mother. He'd have preferred talking to her. They had always talked a lot. But when she wasn't actually around, when she wasn't right there—yelling at him about his messy room or wondering if he was getting along all right with his friends or reminding him that he was one of the new generation of men with what she hoped would be a new attitude to women . . . It was easy to talk with his mother, but he didn't have anything to say to her in a letter, not really. So he was glad the collection was there, to write about to her.

The Egyptian Collection also gave him somewhere to go and something to do. He only went as far as room 015 in the library cellar, and what he did there wasn't much—he just put his hands down into packing straw and pulled up whatever his fingers found—but that little was a little like Christmas, which made it an okay level of fun. It was like a Christmas where nothing was anything you were hoping for, but since everything was wrapped up there was some excitement in finding out what everything was.

Except when Mr. Hall had classes, they spent all day unpacking the collection. Dr. Simard joined them. He'd asked Mr. Hall's permission, as if he were a kid in a TV sitcom asking to use the family car; and Mr. Hall had said yes, as if he were the father and Dr. Simard was the kid. Between his father, and Dr. Simard, and Althea, there wasn't much they didn't know about the pieces in the collection. Phineas felt pretty stupid sometimes, but he didn't mind. Stupid was better than bored, and he was picking up some interesting new words, like wedjat and stela. Wedjat was his favorite, partly because the idea of the two Egyptian gods fighting, and one ripping out the left eye of the other, gave him the shivers. The collection contained what Ken called "a rather fine obsidian wedjat," which stared out at Phineas from the shelf where they had placed it.

Dr. Simard had asked right away if they would all call him Ken, since they were all on the same work crew. Phineas's father was about to object, but Ken looked as if it was something he really, really wanted, so Mr. Hall let it ride. Althea approved, but Phineas wasn't so sure; if grown-ups were equals, then they wouldn't leave you alone to be a kid. But there wasn't anything he could do about it.

In any case, they found out the first day they were unpacking that Ken wasn't going to be around all that much longer. He was going to study in England—"Oxford, I'm pleased to say. They have a papyrus collection I'd like to write a paper on."

"Do you have a grant?" Mr. Hall asked, sounding impressed.

"Unfortunately not. My list of publications is good enough, but when nobodies at Nowhere University are writing your academic recommendations—you don't stand much of a chance, do you?" He gave them no

41

time to answer. "But," with a flash of teeth, "you can't keep a good man down. Isn't that what they say? Our finances permit me to go over for five weeks this summer, so I'm going ahead with the project, grant or no grant."

Phineas held his breath and hoped Ken would stick to the subject of grants and off the subject of papers. He already knew too much about Ken's papers. Ken was only thirty-one, but he'd already published a dozen papers. Just writing the papers didn't count; you had to publish them for them to count. Count for what, Phineas wasn't sure.

"Did you ever publish anything, Dad?" Phineas asked. His father had his hands deep in a crate, and the other three were waiting to see what he'd pull out. Althea was in her usual place on a stool at the end of the table, where she kept a list of what they unpacked, complete with brief descriptions.

"Just a couple of little pieces."

"Time," Ken called, holding his hands up in the familiar coach's signal. "Time, time out here." Phineas couldn't help laughing. "Your father has a way of selling himself short, Phineas," Ken said. "I read one of your papers, Sam, the one in the *Classical Language Journal*. The one on the history of the alpha privative."

"That," Mr. Hall said. He had both hands buried in straw, and pieces of straw in his hair and on his arms. "How did you come across that?"

"The library subscribes to *CLJ*, so when I looked up your publications, I found it. To see what kind of man you were."

"Why would the alpha privative interest you?" Mr. Hall asked, not really paying attention.

"*CLJ* turned down a paper I offered them," Ken said. Phineas was afraid he would tell them all about it, but just then Mr. Hall pulled his hands up out of the straw. One hand held something round and flat and wrapped in cloth. The other hand gradually uncovered it. Ken had stopped speaking, to watch. Phineas caught Ken's mood, like measles, and like Ken he fixed his eyes on his father's hands, on what was about to be revealed.

It was only flowers, just some circle of flowery leafy stuff. It looked like a small Christmas wreath, made out of ivy leaves and little berries. Ken, his father, even Althea, they all just stared at it.

It was in good condition. Phineas guessed that made it different, made it valuable. Besides, the more he looked at the wreath, the more Phineas liked it: The ivy leaves floated as if they were on water, somehow, floating between the clumps of berries that joined the twined leaves, or separated them.

"May I?" Ken asked, holding out his two large hands. "If this is genuine," Ken said, cradling it in his hands, "you have yourself a treasure."

"You mean the college does," Mr. Hall said, in a dreamy and distracted voice.

Phineas looked more carefully. It didn't look like any treasure to him. He wouldn't mind having it in his room, but that didn't make it a treasure. There was lots of stuff in his room nobody would ever call treasure. "What's so special about it?" he asked, figuring that, as usual, there might be something he didn't know that would explain everything.

Ken held the wreath out in front of him. He looked, just for a second—never mind that he was in his gray jogging sweats after his daily six-mile run—he looked like an ancient Viking about to make an offering to his gods. "This is a funerary crown, Phineas. They were used during the Hellenistic period, about five hundred to two hundred B.C. The leaves are ivy, see? But they're

43

wrought in bronze, or so I hope, then gilded. The berries are formed from clay. If it's genuine, it's in remarkably fine condition. Museum condition.''

''Why shouldn't it be genuine?'' Phineas wondered.

''Often wealthy collectors were sold fakes,'' his father said. ''They were sitting ducks for anyone who wanted to bilk them, because they didn't often know anything about what they were buying. This Vandemark man is liable to be a collector like that, in which case all of this may be worthless.''

''That would make Mrs. Batchelor happy,'' Phineas said.

Ken rotated the crown around in his hands, looking at it.

''How do you know if something's fake?'' Phineas asked.

''The papers, the provenance of each item,'' his father told him. ''Expert opinion, if there's any question. You sort of get an eye for what's real, experience, knowledge, the same way—you know when you meet someone if he's honest. I mean, usually you know. Or if she is. Never mind that, you know what I mean. The wreath looks good to me, doesn't it to you, Ken? I assume from its condition that the crowns weren't buried with the bodies,'' Mr. Hall said.

''No.'' Ken couldn't take his eyes off it. Althea got down from her stool to come look more closely at it.

''The Greeks in Egypt cremated their dead, didn't they, Ken?'' Althea asked.

''Very good,'' Ken said, as if she had answered a tough question in class. ''Yes, they did, and the ashes were put into hydra vases, and then these crowns were hung around the necks of the vases. I can't believe I actually have one in my hands. May I have it, Sam?''

''Have it?'' Althea sounded shocked. ''But—''

"Think, Althea," Ken scolded. "If you want to be a scholar, you'll have to learn to think before you speak, in order to avoid sounding like a ninny."

Ken was certainly putting Althea in her place. Phineas wasn't sure how he felt about that. Althea's red cheeks told him how she felt—embarrassed.

"I was about to ask the same question," Mr. Hall said.

"Oh, I'm sorry, Sam, I meant, have it for a paper."

"Sure," Mr. Hall said. "Be my guest."

"I'm serious," Ken said. "If anyone else inquires, you'll tell them it's reserved?"

"You have my word," Mr. Hall said.

"Including—I have to ask—yourself?"

"I'm already too busy. No, listen, you can have it in exchange for the help you're giving me with the collection."

"Wonderful. That's just—wonderful. I tell you, Sam, it's promising for the mummy, isn't it?"

"Why don't we open the mummy crate now?" Phineas suggested. He'd never seen a mummy up close before, but he'd seen plenty of late-night movies.

"Not until Saturday, Phineas," his father reminded him. "That's only one more day, and we'll have everything else uncrated by then. I've arranged with President Blight for a viewing Saturday after lunch. He's having a previewing lunch for certain selected guests. I've also promised O'Meara she can be here. The mummy is the big occasion."

"Phineas doesn't care about the occasion—he's just hoping to be scared out of his wits," Althea said.

She was making Phineas sound bad. He thought of telling her she was wrong, but he figured she was probably right. When he pictured what the mummy would look like, it was pretty horrible, and he could almost feel the chills running up and down his spine. He *was* looking forward to that. Almost as good as a really good roller coaster, that's what he was hoping for, like the Devil's Loop. He'd look at the mummy's face, at its empty eye sockets especially, and his stomach would slam up into his heart. . . .

The Halls spent Saturday morning getting the cellar room ready, sweeping—Phineas's job—and setting out labels on index cards by the artifacts lined up along the double shelves—Althea's and their father's. Then they went home to wash up, become presentable. They returned by 1:15 to the room that now looked, to Phineas's eye anyway, more like a hospital operating room than a workroom. The mummy's crate waited like a coffin on the long table in the center of the room. Behind it, odd shapes and colors lined the shelves. The light was bright and the machinery hummed patiently.

After a while, Ken arrived. Mr. Hall greeted him. "You're dressed up." The Halls wore jeans and sweatshirts. Ken wore white slacks and a long-sleeved knit shirt with a polo player embroidered on its chest.

Ken looked down at himself and you could almost see him deflating. "Do you think I've overdone it? If there's publicity, I wouldn't mind being noticed, and you have to dress for success sometimes." Mr. Hall tried to say something, but Ken talked on. "All of us here know that what a man looks like is no indication of his abilities, but you have to admit we live in an ivory tower." Mr. Hall opened his mouth, but Ken gave him no chance to speak. "Not that I don't like the college, don't get me wrong, but—this isn't Harvard, is it? If I had kids," he added quickly, with a flash of his teeth for Phineas's father, "I'd seriously consider making Vandemark my life work. So maybe it's lucky I don't.

46

Have kids, I mean. My wife doesn't have time for a family anyway. Not with her career as hot as it is. It's no time for her to be starting a family.''

"What's her career?" Phineas asked. A hot career might be something really cool—like a singer or actress. Phineas had never met a real singer, or actress, or anyone married to one.

"Michelle is a stockbroker, with Merrill Lynch."

"Oh."

"She's an incredible woman, Michelle, and charming too—one of the new women, you know. You'd approve of her, Althea, she's impressive. Last year her earnings topped . . ." His voice dribbled off. "I'm sorry, I don't mean to boast, I'm just so proud of her I forget other people might not be interested."

"She sounds successful," Althea observed.

"That she is. And she thrives on success. You probably know what I mean. She's probably a lot like your mom."

None of the Halls had anything to say about that.

"Don't get me wrong, I'm really proud of her."

Phineas hoped Althea would let that pass, but his sister couldn't, of course.

"Is she proud of you?" Althea asked.

"The kitten has claws, doesn't she?" Ken said. His mouth stretched as if he were smiling. "It's open season on men these days, isn't it, Sam?"

"Well," Mr. Hall answered, giving Althea *a look*, "it's not an easy time for marriages. I try to consider it a challenge."

"Sorry," Althea muttered.

"Do you really think we've been that hard on them?" Ken asked. He wasn't asking Althea, Phineas noticed. "Seriously, do you?"

Luckily, at that point they heard footsteps and voices

in the hall, and the clacking sound of high-heeled shoes, so they all turned to greet whoever was arriving.

It was Mrs. Blight, the president's wife, once again all dressed up for the occasion, and once again in the company of the expensively dressed lady. Mrs. Blight introduced the lady as "Mrs. Prynn, who is, as you've probably heard, one of the most involved members of our board of governors." Mrs. Prynn wasn't interested in any of them, except for Mr. Hall.

"You've been given quite a responsibility," she said, as if she doubted his ability to carry it out, especially now that she'd seen him up close.

"Quite an honor," Mr. Hall agreed, agreeably.

Mrs. Prynn looked around the room, not pleased with what she saw. Phineas could see why she might not be. Room 015 was pretty much like a bunker, like the kind of place where Hitler had spent his last days—cement block walls, four bare bulbs hanging down from the ceiling, the metal boxes that were the climate control tucked back into a corner, humming.

"Dear Olivia would never have done it this way," Mrs. Prynn announced, with pursed lips, to Mrs. Blight, who made agreeing murmurs. "Olivia McPhail and I were lifelong friends, Mr. Hall. Lifelong. She would never have assigned any collection she'd gathered to a . . . cellar."

Mrs. Blight murmured excuses.

"Or an entirely inexperienced curator."

Mrs. Blight murmured apologies.

"But isn't that just the way poor Felix always did things?" Mrs. Prynn asked, suddenly cheerful. "He could never admit that he didn't have Olivia's taste, or judgment."

"What judgment?" a man inquired from the doorway, a man of about Mrs. Prynn's age, a fringe of white

48

hair around his head, a portly man in a three-piece pin-striped suit, with a walking stick in his hands, its silver handle carved into a duck's head. "What taste?"

"I might have known you'd be here." Mrs. Prynn's lips were pursed again.

Phineas felt like he was the audience at a tennis match, with his head turning from one to the other of the two.

"You aren't thinking of Olivia's sentimental collection of third-rate watercolors, are you?" the man asked.

Mrs. Prynn sniffed.

"When she could have bought Braque, or Klimt, or Chagall? No, you must be thinking of her investment in the swamplands of northern Florida, another example of her judgment. And business acumen." The man leaned on his walking stick, folding his hands over the duck's head, and—having quelled Mrs. Prynn—asked Mrs. Blight, "Aren't you going to introduce me to the lucky man?"

"Lucky—? Oh, you mean Mr. Hall. Why yes, of course. Sam, this is Calvin Fletcher, another board member."

"Pleased to meet you, Hall, and congratulations. Felix always liked to put his bets on wild cards. You've lucked out on this hand."

"I certainly feel lucky," Phineas's father said.

"Dr. Simard of the History Department, Mr. Fletcher," Ken said, stepping up and holding out his hand. "I don't think we've met. I've been doing what I can to help Sam out down here, using my special knowledge."

Mr. Fletcher shook the hand. "Pleasure. Well. Well? Shall we take a look at this mummy before any more of the afternoon is lost? I'm a busy man. By the way, I approve of the security measures you've taken, Hall, and you've chosen a good climate control system. I'm on the board of the Museum of Fine Arts so I know something about how to handle antiquities." This he said with a glance at Mrs. Prynn, to be sure she was still quelled.

"I do have an afternoon engagement," she answered, as if he had asked. "I have a cocktail party in Kennebunk to get ready for." She smiled a mysterious, hinting smile.

Mr. Hall took a crowbar and started prying at the lid of the crate. The nails creaked, pulling free. "We're going to take the whole box apart," he said, "and packing might fall around—I can't predict." Ken took up another crowbar, to help. The visitors drew back, Mr. Fletcher at the opposite end of the table from Mrs. Prynn, and Mrs. Blight as close to the exact middle point as she could get. As the wooden top creaked free, a voice came out of the corridor—"Wait! Stop!"

O'Meara ran into the room, her dark hair flapping against her cheeks, her sandles flapping against the floor. "I'm sorry. I got lost—this is a real rabbit warren down here." Her camera was up and she was taking pictures. "Did I miss anything?" She came up to the table and looked into the box. "It's gone! There's nothing but straw here!" She looked slowly from one of them to the other, a complete circle. "Did someone steal it?" she whispered. "Or—"

Mr. Hall cleared his throat, and set the lid down on the floor. "Miss O'Meara—"

"No Miss, no Ms., I *told* you. Just O'Meara. I don't want to run into any more of that sexist garbage than I have to. What's wrong here? What's happened?"

"We were just taking the top off the mummy's crate," Mr. Hall continued, patiently. "Like everything else in the collection, the mummy is packed in straw.

O'Meara,'' he explained to the two board members, ''is covering this event for the *Post*.''

''Then I can get pictures of everything, every step.'' That cheered O'Meara up. She got her camera ready.

Phineas didn't have any part to play in all of this, but he was having a pretty good time. He always enjoyed it when grown-ups acted like jerks, and a lot of the grown-ups present were acting like serious jerks. He stood back and enjoyed himself.

Ken and Mr. Hall set to work on the sides of the crate with their crowbars. O'Meara wanted to know why they were doing that, and they explained that they didn't want to risk damaging the mummy and that they didn't know what kind of condition it was in. She took out her notebook and wrote that down. She said she thought mummies were mummified, and pretty tough, practically petrified after all this time. Ken explained that this was a Roman era mummy, when the funerary arts had degenerated. She wrote that down. When was the Roman era? she wondered. Both men were busy with crowbars, so Althea told her first to fourth centuries, A.D., roughly, and O'Meara wrote that down. Why was it called the Roman era when it was in Egypt? she wondered.

Wooden slats were piling up on the floor. Clumps of dry straw were falling down from the table. With the long sides off, the crate looked almost like a bed, with headboard and footboard, and a long mound of straw between them. O'Meara took some pictures. The two men pried at the ends to work them free of the crate's bottom. More straw fell down, but everyone came close anyway.

''Althea? Phineas?'' their father asked. ''Help with the straw, will you please?—but carefully. We don't know exactly what we'll find.''

51

Phineas pulled gently at clumps of straw, up near where the head would be, he hoped. He made himself concentrate on the straw and the mounded shape within it, to push away his consciousness of the other people in the room and be alone with his first glimpse of the mummy. With its arms and chest wrapped as if with bandages, and its head, and its eyes—

At last the mummy lay uncovered.

Phineas and the others gathered around the table, like guests at a Thanksgiving dinner, and nobody said a word. Phineas was so busy looking that he didn't have any words to speak.

The mummy lay on the table like a giant cocoon, wrapped around and around with strips of what appeared to be cloth—brown in places, creamy white in places—that had been wound into diamond-shaped designs all up and down the body.

The hairs at the back of Phineas's neck prickled.

The mummy was hundreds of years dead and it seemed to be breathing out hundreds of years of death into the tomblike room. It seemed old in a way none of the other artifacts on the shelves were, maybe because it had once been human like everybody in the room, but maybe because its face looked out at them with big, sad eyes.

Not its mummy face. A portrait. That was worse than a dried-up face, because the portrait looked like a real person, who had a real life, and a name, just like each one of them had.

Phineas couldn't take his eyes off it. It was horrible, and wonderful. The shape under the wrappings couldn't be anything but human—the rounded head, broader shoulders and chest, narrowing down to hips and then knees and then ankles, with what had to be feet sticking straight up at the end. He would have liked it better without the portrait, with the face just diamond-shaped wrappings. Without the portrait it was a mummy. But the portrait told you it was a person, somebody particular.

O'Meara broke the silence. "It's a girl."

Althea had tears in her eyes. Phineas didn't blame her, looking down the length of the mummy to where his sister stood at her feet. He almost felt like crying himself, looking at the girl's face in the portrait, her dark hair curled along her forehead under a wreath of flowers she wore like a crown, her sad brown eyes that looked right at him. Her skin looked like real skin, and her mouth was pink, and she had a little dimple in her right cheek, as if she was trying not to laugh. A heavy gold necklace with dark stones embedded in it circled her neck, and the dress she wore, of which all that showed was the top, was purple. He wondered what her name was, and why she had died when she was still so young, and how her eyes could look so sad even while her mouth looked like it was about to laugh.

✶ 6 ✶

FOR A MINUTE, PHINEAS FORGOT WHO HE WAS.

The only sound was the hum of machinery. Beyond the open door, a maze of corridors and rooms and closets seemed to echo silence, almost as if Phineas were an archaeologist standing in the burial room of an actual tomb. Or even, for that minute, as if he were an ancient Egyptian, bidding a last farewell to the dead girl before he turned around to wind his way up, through twisting passages, to the clear desert air.

Phineas looked across the table, across the mummy's face, to his father. Mr. Hall stared down at the wrapped figure, and at the portrait face that was held in place by wrappings, and then back down the length of the mummy to its feet, where Althea stood staring.

Phineas guessed he finally knew how his father felt. He'd never understood before how anything so old and long gone as the languages and books his father studied, and taught, and talked about, could be important. He wasn't sure he exactly understood that now, but he felt as if this ancient mummy stood for something truer than . . . all the money he could imagine winning in the lottery, truer than Donald Trump, truer even than the threat of nuclear war and nuclear accidents, AIDS, or the waste crisis. If he could understand what the mummy had to say to him—only she would speak in Egyptian, wouldn't she, or Latin, so even if she could speak he wouldn't be able to understand her. But if he could—

Everybody else was feeling about the same, Phineas thought, Althea wiping her eyes on the sleeve of her sweatshirt and Ken peering down at the wrappings the way dogs looked at bowls of food in TV advertisements. O'Meara was looking from the mummy's face to his father's face, as if Phineas's father had somehow gotten all the credit and responsibility for the mummy, at least in her mind. Mr. Fletcher was nodding his head, with a little I-told-you-so smile on his mouth for Mrs. Prynn, who was pursing her lips at the mummy, trying to look unimpressed. Mrs. Blight stood between them, looking from each of their faces to the mummy's face, as if one of the three could tell her how she should react.

"Well," Mr. Hall said, and he laughed out loud. "Wow," he said. "Oh—wow."

That broke the stunned silence.

"Can I take pictures?" O'Meara asked, and had her camera to her eye, clicking and forwarding film, before anyone could answer. She photographed the mummy first, from above and from the sides, and then the people standing around, and then she went out to the hallway to photograph the room from the outside. While she took pictures she asked questions. Mr. Hall and Ken took turns answering them, and the other visitors looked over the artifacts on the shelves and had questions of their own. Neither Phineas nor Althea had anything to say, nor did they have any desire to move from where they stood at the head and foot of the mummy.

"How old was she?" O'Meara asked.

"She doesn't look anything over fifteen," Mr. Hall said.

"Although the mummy herself might be much older," Ken added. "Often, portraits were painted years before they were needed. Probably hung for decoration in homes, waiting until the subject died.''

"That's not a very pleasant idea,'' Mrs. Prynn observed. "It wouldn't be my idea of attractive interior decor.''

"And that sheet it's lying on, is that an original Egyptian sheet?'' O'Meara asked.

Now that she mentioned it, Phineas could see that the mummy lay on a single sheet that had been brought up over her shoulders and part of her feet, and sides.

"Yes. A kind of partial shroud,'' Ken said.

"Well,'' Mrs. Prynn announced, "Felix certainly didn't take very good care of it. Which is no surprise to those of us who knew him. Look at those stains— and that looks like graffiti on the wrappings.''

"Sometimes sealing resins soak through the wrappings,'' Mr. Hall told her. "Remember, this was done at least fifteen hundred years ago, and at a time when the funerary arts were in decline. You wouldn't expect mint condition.''

"It looks like my dining room ceiling when the bathroom pipes gave out,'' Mrs. Prynn insisted. "It looks to me as if Felix got himself a pig in a poke.''

"Not likely,'' Mr. Fletcher said. He harrumphed over by the shelves. "The old man wasn't the fool you women liked to make him out to be.''

"This is no fake,'' Ken announced.

"You're sure of that?'' O'Meara asked.

"As a scholar, I have to wait for the results of certain tests to be absolutely sure. You should know that. But''—Ken put his hand up so she would let him finish what he was saying—"I've read Petrie, the great nineteenth-century Egyptologist, you know, who was the first to do carefully documented exhumations of the Roman era cemeteries—and this tallies with his descriptions."

"Is she wearing that necklace?" O'Meara asked. "It looks like gold, but what are those stones?"

"Probably uncut emeralds." Ken didn't even look up from the mummy to answer. "Emeralds were common, at the time. But at that time, it wasn't usual to bury jewels, or anything else, with the dead."

"You can't say for sure though, can you?" O'Meara asked, writing away.

"I can't, without an X ray," Ken agreed.

Phineas had gotten over the first shock of the mummy and was happily watching what everyone else got up to. Sometimes, he thought he'd like to have the talent to be a cartoonist. If adults knew what they looked and sounded like. . . .

"Ken," Althea said, "are those hieroglyphs?"

Ken moved to stand beside her and bend down over the feet.

"I wouldn't be surprised."

"But those," she pointed, "look like Greek. A kappa, isn't it?"

Ken bent closer. He took his time, being careful. "No."

"But, here, look. Isn't that kappa, lambda, epsilon—"

Ken interrupted her. "I don't see anything remotely resembling those letters."

"But—"

"No," he said again. "I'm sorry to disappoint you. I've studied hieroglyphs," he reminded her. "These look demotic—later corruptions I'd guess—but characteristic. I know you've got younger eyes, I know you'd like to make a discovery, but I'm afraid you're mistaking demotic hieroglyphs of a language in decline for something they aren't. That's how it looks to my experienced eyes. I can see what's probably ankh, mew, smir—that's courtier. A courtier living by the water? I'd have to study it. I can't pretend to sightread hieroglyphs, but everyone knows what ankh looks like."

Althea pressed her lips together.

"Why would anyone write on mummy wrappings?" Mr. Fletcher asked. "Seems pointless—unless, did they write prayers on them? Or magic spells?" Mrs. Prynn turned around from her examination of the funeral wreath to sniff. "There were spells to keep intruders out," Mr. Fletcher said to her, "to keep the mummy safe. The spirit's home was in the mummy, and if the mummy was destroyed the spirit was homeless. Anyone who has even the slightest knowledge of Egyptology knows that."

Mrs. Prynn sniffed again and turned her back to him. Mr. Fletcher humphed.

"Actually, it wasn't that they wrote on the wrappings," Mr. Hall answered him. "Sometimes they did, although the usual practice was to wrap a copy of prayers, or the book of the dead, in with the body. But most often, at this time, instead of traditional linen, they used strips of papyrus for the wrappings—rather like we use newspaper to make papier-mâché. Think of it as ancient recycling."

Phineas grinned.

"Especially," Mr. Hall continued, "after Christianity began to spread. Some of the pagan writers were acceptable to Christians—Plato for example, and Virgil—which is why so many of their works are available to us. But the others, who were a majority—like your Sappho, Althea, she's a good example, because the early Christians used her as an example of everything sensual and sinful in the classical world. In fact, the bishop of Constantinople ordered all of Sappho's writings burned.

Sappho wasn't the only pagan they disapproved of either, not by a long shot. There were dozens of writers, some of them we'll never see even a line of their work. However," he concluded his little lecture, "frequently the destruction of undesirable books took the form of ripping the papyruses into strips, for use as mummy wrappings."

"I didn't know you'd done work in history, as well as languages," Ken observed.

"Oh I didn't, or, not much. I've been reading up on Egypt. You don't imagine that I'm the only person who doesn't know I'm underqualified for this position, do you? But I intend to do as good a job as I can."

"Now that's the kind of thinking I like to hear," Mr. Fletcher said.

"Nobody is blaming you," Mrs. Blight assured Mr. Hall.

"I blame Felix," Mrs. Prynn announced. "And I plan to talk with the family about proper placement of the collection," she told Mr. Fletcher.

"You can tell them they aren't going to get their hands on it," Mr. Fletcher answered. "I drew up that will. It's safe."

She sniffed.

"Although I'll enjoy watching you vultures try to disqualify it. That'll cost you a pretty penny."

Phineas tried to catch Althea's eye.

"Dear Olivia would have done it properly," Mrs. Prynn said, "and not by hiring some unqualified young man as curator—nothing personal," she said to Mr. Hall, "I'm sure you're quite good in your own field."

"In the meantime," Mrs. Blight said, in a peacemaker's voice, the kind that suggested cups of tea, before Phineas's father could say anything.

But she never finished her sentence. They heard

59

voices in the corridor, a deep, woman's voice and the nasal voice of a man. Sound traveled faster than feet along the corridors. The voices sounded clear, but far away. Everybody in the room listened.

"What is it?" O'Meara whispered. "It sounds almost ghostly."

"Undead creatures called forth by the mummy's curse," Mr. Hall told her.

"What curse?" Mrs. Prynn demanded.

"I like it," O'Meara laughed.

Mrs. Prynn went on. "There is no curse. There was never the hint of a curse. If that's the college's attitude, I don't think the family will have any difficulty removing the collection from Vandemark."

"Of course there isn't a curse," Ken said.

The voices floating down the corridor grew fainter.

"But I heard what he said, you heard him—"

"He was joking," Ken explained.

Mrs. Prynn turned to study Phineas's father, and clearly did not like what she saw.

Phineas bit the inside of his cheek to keep from laughing.

The voices grew louder, clear and unghostlike, and then Mrs. Batchelor entered the room, followed by her husband. She strode right up to Mrs. Blight to say, "The president kindly invited my husband to the unveiling. You remember Mark, of course," she added, as if, Phineas thought, nobody could forget him. "I hope we're not too late?"

Mr. Batchelor looked more like a New Yorker than anybody else in the room, and acted it too, as he introduced himself to those he'd never met, "Mark Batchelor, Lucille's husband, I'm employed at the museum," and said hello to those he already knew, "Ken, how's Michelle? Mrs. Prynn, I always enjoy seeing you." But he was impatient to look at the collection, and it was the mummy he stood over first. Everybody waited for what he would say, as he bent over the mummy. But he said nothing. He just turned to the shelves, and moved slowly along them, his face without expression. Still, the room awaited whatever words he would choose to speak.

"Nothing to be ashamed of about this," Mr. Batchelor finally said. "You're right to be concerned, Lucille."

"I thought so. I knew it. What do you think the library should do?"

"The mummy isn't a bad one either."

Not bad? The mummy? The mummy was miles better than not bad. Even Phineas could see that.

"You know of course what the gemstone is?" Mr. Batchelor didn't sound as if he thought they knew anything. "The wreath."

"Gemstone?" O'Meara asked, moving over to point her camera at the wreath. "Are the berries rubies?"

"I spoke metaphorically," Mr. Batchelor said.

O'Meara nodded her head and clicked her camera.

"Only if it's proved genuine," Mrs. Prynn pointed out at the same time that Mr. Fletcher asked, "What kind of value would you put on it?"

Mr. Batchelor talked on, dropping hints about all the important museums he'd been in, not exactly saying he'd worked there but implying that he might have. "At the Met, they maintain a temperature of . . . The Egyptology section of the Reading Room at the British . . . When I was preparing a monograph in Cairo . . ." He offered his help in arranging to have the mummy X-rayed: "You plan to do that, of course, it's standard practice"; he offered transportation in one of the museum's vans; he offered to send the official museum

61

photographer over, for insurance records; he said he didn't know if he could promise but he'd be glad to inquire about the possibility of transferring the wreath— "We wouldn't want to give room to the entire collection, of course"—to one of the museum's storage rooms. "You've done well by way of security, with your limited resources," Mr. Batchelor said, making it sound like Mr. Hall hadn't done well enough. "If I can be of help, you'll be sure to let me know? Any advice—since I gather from my wife you have no experience, have had no training—"

Mrs. Batchelor seconded her husband's opinion. "I'm not happy having something like that in the library, especially now that I know it's valuable."

"Anything at all I can help you with, I'd be glad to. Do think over my offer to take the wreath. If anything were to happen to it . . ." He let them imagine all the things that might happen, and what would be the consequences of that. He left the room, his wife following behind asking, "You don't think anything *will* happen, do you?"

For a few minutes, everybody had to stare at the wreath, which nobody had paid much attention to before, and then finally they began to leave. And about time, Phineas thought. O'Meara was the last to go, and she lingered at the doorway.

"I for one wish there was some kind of curse," she said.

"I'm sure there is none. And you can quote me," Ken answered.

"It would make such a good story," O'Meara said, and left the room.

Ken looked at his watch. "I have to go," he said, sounding surprised. "I'm sorry, Sam, I had no idea how long—The thing is, one of Michelle's clients has invited us for a supper sail, I promised I'd be home and ready to go at three-thirty—''

"Go ahead. We're just going to close up in here and be right behind you. You don't want to be late.''

When they were alone, however, they spent a few minutes looking down at the mummy. "I don't care what that man says," Mr. Hall told his children, "I don't care if he's right either, although I never take experts on faith—she's the gemstone. Show me your Greek, Althea, what you thought was.''

Althea shook her head. "Never mind. Ken's probably right—I was just—you know how it is, Dad.''

"Yes, I do.''

His father wasn't curious, but Phineas was. He went around to look at the mummy's feet. The markings looked like chicken scratches to him. They didn't look like anything. He didn't say that. What he said was, "Do we know her name?''

"I wish we did. I'd like to have a name for her,'' Mr. Hall said. "She looks so . . .''

"As if she had a name,'' Althea finished.

"Yeah,'' Phineas said. "Maybe it'll be somewhere in the papers?'' he suggested. "The ones Mr. Vandemark gave you?''

They went out into the corridor. Mr. Hall locked the door with a big key, then flipped a light switch just under the room number painted on the wall.

Nothing happened.

Mr. Hall acted as if nothing happening was what was supposed to happen.

"What's that, Dad?'' Phineas asked. "That switch,'' he said, when it looked like his father was going to try a bluff.

"Oh, that? That's just—Dan Lewis, who's in charge of security, recommended a little something extra.
63

We've put in an electric circuit that's completed when the door is closed. If it's broken, without the power being turned off, an alarm sounds in the guard's office at the main gate. Nobody knows about it, except Dan Lewis, and me, and now you two. So don't tell anyone.''

''Who would we tell?'' Althea asked.

''Who would want to know?'' Phineas reassured him.

❦ 7 ❦

THE MUMMY'S DARK EYES STARED OUT FROM THE front page of Monday's newspaper. The portrait was identified in the caption as a "Roman Mummy, circa first to fourth century, now at Vandemark College."

Phineas figured he must have gotten something wrong. "I didn't realize she was a Roman," he said.

"Don't be dumb, Phineas," Althea advised him. She was standing behind his left shoulder, to read over it. His father stood at his right shoulder for the same purpose. "The Romans didn't mummify their dead."

When Phineas pointed to the caption, Althea laughed.

"You believe everything you read? In the newspaper? In an article by O'Meara? When you know she has the mind of a chicken?"

"How do you know what kind of a mind a chicken has?" Phineas demanded. He got tired of being put down, just because he wasn't a bookworm, just because he wasn't as old as she was, just because he was a boy. He didn't know why, exactly, she kept putting him down, but he didn't like her doing it. Who said she knew everything anyway? "Chickens might be really smart, for all you know, like those mice in the *Hitchhiker's Guide* books." Phineas grinned. Althea refused to read those books because they were so popular. Anything everybody can like has to be inferior: That was her opinion. So she couldn't beat his argument this time. "Isn't that right, Dad?"

"Don't try to drag me into it," his father said, without looking up from his reading.

"O'Meara should have said Roman *era*," Althea explained to him. "When Egypt was part of the Roman Empire—like Greece was, and France, and England too."

The trouble with Althea was, once she got started showing off how much she knew about something, she could go on forever. "I'm trying to read," Phineas said. He didn't blame her for wanting to talk about how much she knew. He just didn't want to have to listen to her. "I can't read when you talk," he pointed out.

He read. They read over his shoulders.

TREASURES GO TO COLLEGE was the headline. As a joke, Phineas thought, it was seriously pitiful.

Egyptian Antiquities Left to Vandemark College by Son of Founder, was the first subheading. First a lie, to catch your eye, then the truth . . . he tried to find a rhyming line for the poem he'd stumbled upon in his own head. Truth-Ruth-Duluth. Uncouth, youth, but not mouth. His mind finished the poem despite his advice: First a lie to catch your eye, then the truth to shut your mouth. But that didn't make sense. All of this happened within Phineas's head in a millisecond, and was done and gone before he really noticed anything.

He read on:

President Ernest S. Blight of Vandemark College has announced the gift of his Egyptian Collection by the late Felix K. C. Vandemark II to the college his father founded in 1897. The bequest includes not only the antiquities themselves but also a fund earmarked for the construction of a room to display the collection. Samuel Hall of the Classical Languages Department will oversee the collection. "When the addition to the library is built," President Blight says, "we hope the people of Portland will be frequent visitors."

The antiquities were acquired by Felix K. C. Vandemark II during his time in Egypt, 1915–1919, and had been privately stored until their unveiling, last Saturday, at the college. Felix K. C. Vandemark IV accompanied the treasures on their journey to their new home. "Grandfather bought whatever caught his eye, or caught his fancy," Mr. Vandemark said. "The exact value of the collection, monetary or historical, cannot be established at this time."

Professor Can't Swear That Treasures Are Genuine

The showpiece of the collection, which also includes scarabs, canopic jars, and a wreath of leaves and berries that has been offered room at the Portland Museum, is a mummy of the Roman era (A.D. 1–4 century) of the kind known as a portrait mummy, because its face is covered by a portrait of the deceased. The portrait depicts a young woman wearing a necklace of uncut emeralds set in heavy gold. "Until we've studied the provenance papers and had some fairly simple tests run," a member of the college community remarked, "we can't be certain just what we have here, of what quality or value.

"The collection will first be cataloged, while the wing to house it is being designed and built," he added. "At first glance, I can say only that it seems to have no single historical focus. Of course, Mr. Vandemark was an amateur. On the other hand, we must remember that many of the great nineteenth-century Egyptologists were also amateurs."

Professor Denies Mummy's Curse

The mummy presently lies on a table in a room deep in the cellars of the college library. This is the first time it has been uncrated since the late Mr. Vandemark brought it back from Egypt, 70 years ago. It was stored in a specially built wooden crate, packed around with straw to prevent damage.

When, where, from whom, and for how much, the mummy was purchased will not be known until the credentials that accompanied the collection to Portland have been thoroughly gone over. Until then, the mummy remains shrouded in mystery.

Security Is Adequate, Spokesman Says

Representatives of the college and the Portland Museum were all present for the unveiling of the antiquities. Mark Batchelor, assistant director of the museum, inquired about the security arrangements and Mr. Hall, curator of the collection, assured him that they were adequate.

The collection is presently being kept in a windowless room in the cellar of the college library. Climate and temperature control systems have been installed. The building is locked at all times when it is not in use. The college also maintains a 24-hour security watch over the campus. "The whole city will benefit from this gift," President Blight said. "I'm sure that was in Mr. Vandemark's mind when he decided to honor the college with the collection."

The front page picture was the mummy, her face turned into grainy black and white. One picture on the back pages, accompanying the continuation of O'Meara's article, showed the storage room seen from the corridor, the open doorway framing a picture within, with vague shapes on shelves, and the mummy lying on its table. Another was a photograph of the group standing around the table ("Those present include Samuel Hall, far right, and Mark Batchelor, of the Portland

Museum, second from left."). The third was of the artifacts on the shelves, with the wreath at its center ("Artifacts that accompanied the mummy on her long journey. The funeral wreath was described by Mr. Batchelor as priceless.").

Phineas's father groaned aloud as he read the article. He swore aloud when he'd finished.

"She didn't quote you at all," Althea said to her father.

"Maybe I'm not quotable."

"She quoted Ken."

"What upsets me is that the woman has as good as given a map. The room number is the clearest thing in any of these misbegotten photographs."

"You actually think somebody would want to steal the stuff?" Phineas asked.

"I can't imagine it, not seriously," his father answered. "Who'd want a mummy. I mean, what would you do with it? It's not as if you could hang it over the fireplace like a Picasso. There's not much of a market for stolen mummies, not like cameras, VCRs, cars. But I don't like it."

"What about the wreath?" Althea asked. "They keep saying how valuable it is."

Phineas was more interested in who would want to steal a mummy. "What about devil worshipers? I bet they'd love to get their hands on a body. Or a grave robber? Schools use bodies for science don't they? Or, aren't there people who just like dead bodies? There are, like people who have a thing about shoes, body fetishists." Now he started to think of it, he could think of a hundred reasons for someone to steal the mummy.

"I don't like it," Mr. Hall repeated.

"I don't like Ken," Althea offered.

"I don't mind him," Phineas said. "But then," he

needled, "he didn't put me down like he did you." The truth was, sometimes Althea needed a little squashing.

"I'm glad we didn't tell O'Meara about the alarm," Mr. Hall said. "If we had, she would probably have made that her headline, with a diagram and instructions for how to turn it off."

"I wouldn't worry, Dad. Anyone who didn't know his way around down there couldn't even find the room. The room numbers don't follow any pattern," Althea offered.

"But the number is there, by the door." Mr. Hall couldn't be comforted.

"We could guard it if you want," Phineas offered. "We could camp out there, taking watches, in our sleeping bags." He thought that might be fun, and scary down there in the dark, mazelike corridors.

"Speak for yourself, Phineas. You wouldn't catch me doing that," Althea said.

"We're being irrational," their father announced. "Only an expert would be interested in the collection, and an expert would know it's not worth stealing. We've got locks, we've got an alarm system, we don't need to worry."

Phineas was a little disappointed to hear that.

✖ 8 ✖

THE SOUND SLAMMED UP AGAINST THE DARKNESS.

Phineas was out of bed, out of the room, halfway down the stairs before it came again. *Blatt-blatt.*

It was the phone. Up in Maine, phones didn't ring. Instead, they blatted, like a double raspberry, *blatt-blatt*. It was the middle of the night, it was dark, who would call in the middle of the night? Bad news. Seriously bad news.

Phineas stopped where he was, halfway down the stairs. His heart pounded but his feet stayed put. He wasn't about to go down there and pick up the phone and hear what the bad news was.

Blatt-blatt.

He didn't know where his mother was. He didn't even know what time it was where she was.

His father thudded past him, down the stairs. *Blatt—* "Hello . . . Dan, yes."

A light came on in the upstairs hallway, and Phineas could see the railing, his father's naked back and rumpled boxers, the black telephone hunched on its table.

"You're kidding," Mr. Hall said. His fingers scratched at his frizzy hair. "But why would anyone?"

Althea had stopped to put on her bathrobe over the flannel nightgown, and her slippers. The light in her room would have already been on, because Althea always slept with the light on. The switch for the hall light was right outside her door, so she'd turned it on, on her way to join Phineas, so she wouldn't ever have to be in darkness.

"No, I'll be right over," their father said. Althea sat on the step beside Phineas. "I won't be able to get back to sleep anyway," Mr. Hall said. He turned around and saw his children watching him. "Everything's okay," he told them. "No, talking to my kids. Just give me a couple of minutes to get dressed. I'm glad you called me."

"What time—" Althea wondered.

"Three," Phineas answered without thinking. He wondered if he was right. He'd never tested his time sense in the middle of the night. Althea was the one who slept restlessly, and had bad dreams. Phineas put his head on the pillow, and was out until hunger, or the alarm, woke him.

"I'll be with you shortly," Mr. Hall said. He hung up the receiver and turned around. "That's enough to give a man a cardiac arrest."

"What happened?" Althea asked.

"I thought—" Phineas started to say.

"Me too," his father said. Then he laughed. "We could call her, to make ourselves feel better, but we'd probably wake her up, and scare her out of her wits too."

"Who was that?" Althea asked.

"Dan Lewis, head of security. Somebody, apparently, tried to break into room oh-fifteen. Dan said it looks like the alarms chased off whoever it was. Nothing's been taken."

"Is he sure?"

"That's why I'm going over."

"Me too," Althea said. She ran up the stairs.

"I'll get my shoes," Phineas said. He slept in his clothes, so shoes were the only thing he was missing.

72

"There's no need," his father said.

"Yeah but I want to," Phineas said. He didn't want to be left out of the excitement, if there was any.

They drove to the library and parked by the rear entrance. Mr. Hall had brought along his big flashlight, because the library lights were automatically turned off at night. A man waited in the yellow light by the door. He was a slight man, in a gray uniform that looked like a police uniform but wasn't. He had gray hair, in a military cut, and stood with a soldier's erectness.

"Phineas, Althea—Mr. Lewis," Mr. Hall introduced them. "Shall we take a look? The kids have worked with the collection from the start, Dan."

"Well"—he considered Althea and Phineas and made up his mind—"I guess it's okay. I've been through the whole place, and it looks like he's long gone. Come on in, Professor, kids. I've got the lights switched on, so you won't need that flashlight."

"I'm not a professor," Mr. Hall said, "just an instructor. Call me Sam." He led the way inside.

Lights shone in the corridors, and they hurried along, turning left, turning right, turning left and then right again. At the door, they all stopped. The door was just slightly ajar. On the door itself, and on the frame, there were concave dents, like a car after a fender bender.

"I figure, he must have used a crowbar. The same kind of marks are on the door from the library."

"So he got back into the cellar from inside the library?" Althea asked. "How did he get in the library?"

"Good thinking, young lady. A window, it must have been left unlocked, open, into the reading room."

"Well," Mr. Hall said, and pushed with his shoulder

73

against the door. It swung open. He pulled his sweat-shirt down over his hand to switch on the light.

At first glance, the room looked exactly the way they'd left it the evening before. The mummy lay on her table, the artifacts were lined up on the shelves. While his father and sister went to look at the shelves, Phineas checked on the mummy. She looked up at him, with her sad little smile. She hadn't been touched.

"I think the alarm probably scared him off," Mr. Lewis said from the door. "Everything present and accounted for, Pro—Sam?"

"As far as I can tell. Althea?"

She nodded.

"It took me maybe five minutes to get over here once the alarm sounded in the office. I figure he's long gone."

"If the door was like that, he probably never even went inside," Phineas said.

"My guess exactly," Mr. Lewis said. "Of course, I could be surprised. I've been surprised a few times in my life."

"I thought things were pretty crime free up here," Phineas said. "Who do you think—?"

Mr. Lewis shook his head. "No idea."

"It's a good thing you put in that alarm," Althea said.

"It's an even better thing only the four of us knew about it," her father answered.

"You two kids," Mr. Lewis said, "why don't you go back to bed, now you've seen what there is to see?"

Phineas hesitated. He would rather have stayed, to find out what it was like being questioned by the police. One look at Mr. Lewis's face, however, convinced him that it was a good idea to go back home. Mr. Lewis was looking him straight in the eye, waiting to be

74

obeyed. He looked like the kind of man accustomed to having people do what he told them.

Mr. Lewis thought he was hesitating for a different reason. "You'll be perfectly safe, walking back. You'll be fine alone in the house."

"That wasn't—" Phineas didn't want Mr. Lewis thinking he was afraid, but his father cut him off.

"Tell me something, Dan, why is it that everyone seems to know all about my private life? I haven't even been here four weeks."

"Is that getting to you?" Mr. Lewis asked. "If it is, my advice is, you better get used to it. Vandemark's a small place. You show up with two kids and no wife— or wife equivalent these days—and people want to know why. If it helps, the gossip's mostly done with good intentions. There's never more than just a little spicing of malice."

The two men looked at one another, and laughed. "Okay," Mr. Hall said. "Then how about you? How long have you been here? I know you're ex-service, but what else is there? A family? Where did you serve? What branch were you in?"

Phineas and Althea left them to it.

They walked across the empty campus without speaking. Phineas wasn't sleepy, just the opposite. The night silence, the trees looming over the deserted pathway, the vast dark sky full of stars—it all made him feel as if something was about to happen, and he was ready for it.

When they got home, Althea went straight to the kitchen. She took down two mugs and the box of cocoa mix, put milk on to heat, and emptied two packets into the mugs. "Incredible cocoa," she read from the box. "I'm going to write them a letter."

75

Phineas looked at her.

"I am. I want credible cocoa, real cocoa—think about it, Phineas. Don't you ever think about that? Incredible cocoa—you know what that is?"

Phineas shook his head.

Althea stared at him. She didn't say a word. She didn't say anything, but all the words she wasn't saying seemed to be crowding up inside her mouth, trying to get out, like lava trying to find the weak spot in a volcano's surface. She turned her back on him and poured the milk into the mugs. Phineas accepted his and blew across the top, sniffed in the chocolaty-milky smell, and waited for whatever was bothering Althea.

"You never say anything," finally burst out of her.

Phineas knew what she meant. He had thought that was it. He wished the phone would ring again, or the police would come to ask them questions, anything for her to use this worked-up excitement on. Althea wanted to talk, but she'd just try to blame someone, and work herself up to anger; then she'd probably cry and run out of the room. He had to say something. "Lay off, Althea, would you? Please? I'm twelve years old—I break things and my feet smell and teachers yell at me—what is there for me to say?"

"I mean Mom."

He knew that.

"You don't *do* anything."

"What could I do?" he asked. "Nobody can *do* anything. And who're you to talk? All you've done is bury your face in some book. Some Greek book."

"She shouldn't be doing it. It isn't as if he hasn't always let her run things before. Do you imagine that he wanted to teach high school? He's got a PhD, Phineas."

"He liked teaching high school," Phineas protested.

76

"He always likes things, that's the way he is. That doesn't excuse her. She should have come along, when he got this job. He always went along with her for her jobs."

"So you blame her."

"Don't you?"

Phineas shook his head. "No." He figured, his mother got tired of having them around to pick up after and nag, to make up her second full-time job. She'd said that pretty often, about having two full-time jobs, and he'd never let it get through to him; he figured, she was a grown-up, she knew what she was doing, if she didn't like it she could take care of it herself. He was sorry, and he wished now he had tried to help out instead of trying to get away with not doing things, but he didn't blame his mother. "You don't understand."

"Just because you look like her doesn't mean you can read her mind. How do you think Dad feels, having to explain to people? Do you ever think about that?"

"Look, Althea," Phineas said. He couldn't believe that she didn't already know this. She was the smart one. "It doesn't have anything to do with us. It's not our marriage, and we can't do anything about it. It's not even our business," he pointed out. "We're just kids."

Althea was looking thoughtfully at him. He lifted his mug and drank down some cocoa, so he wouldn't have to look back at her. "Sappho was a woman," Althea said.

What was that supposed to mean?

"Tradition says she was married, to a merchant, a businessman. She definitely had a daughter, named Kleis. That's proved by her poems. There are also stories that she was a lesbian—she lived on Lesbos, and

77

that's where the name comes from, from Sappho of Lesbos. There's proof for that in the poems too."

So what? Phineas wondered, and drank. "Are you saying you think Mom's gay?"

"You take everything so personally, that isn't—I'm trying to say that it must have been a lot the same for her," Althea said. "Conflicts and choices. I'm trying to say maybe it isn't all that different now. Nothing much has changed for women." She waited. "You must think something, Fin—what do you think about that?"

"If that's true, it's pretty depressing," Phineas said.

"If it's true, I guess it could be depressing. Except— Sappho's a great poet, everybody agrees, so something worked right in her life. I don't know if Mom is right about taking the job, I don't even know if I'm so sure she's wrong. That's depressing too." She drank her cocoa, looking at him but not seeing him. Phineas let his mind drift, now that she wasn't going to blow up at him. "Who *do* you think did it?" she asked.

"Huh? Did what?"

"Broke into the collection."

"How would I know?"

"You wouldn't, I didn't ask you if you knew. I just asked you who you thought. We could probably figure it out."

"Why us?"

"Because," Althea explained, "we're on the scene. We know as much as anyone else. Except whoever did it."

"Who'd want to?" Phineas asked, meaning he couldn't imagine who would want to take the collection or any part of it.

Althea took that as a real question. "That's a good idea. Motive. If we think about who might want to steal something, then you narrow down the possibilities.

78

Somebody who thought something in there was worth stealing. Somebody who read that article in the paper and thought the emerald necklace was inside the mummy?''

"But Ken said it wasn't. He said they didn't bury people with their jewels on, then.''

"So someone who didn't know that. Unless,'' Althea said, "our mummy is an exception, and she *is* wearing the necklace.''

"That would show up in an X ray,'' Phineas said. "Dad's going to have X rays done.''

"So we'll find out, pretty soon. Ken acts like he knows everything, but he could be wrong.''

"I bet it was just some kids. Some kids who read the article in the paper and don't have anything better to do, just seeing if they could get in. That sounds likely, doesn't it?''

"It does to me,'' Althea said, sipping thoughtfully, "but that could just be because I'm a kid. It's easier to imagine why someone who's like you would do something, even if it's something you'd never do. I bet neither Dad nor Mr. Lewis have thought of kids. I wonder if the police will.''

It was kind of fun, thinking up all the possibilities. "Wait,'' Phineas asked, getting up. "Let me get paper.''

"Why?''

"To write things down. We can make a list.'' Althea made a face. "Yeah, but if we write it down, then we'll avoid repeating ideas.''

"Mr. Efficiency,'' she said, but she waited.

"First, a thief,'' Phineas said, writing that down. "To steal the necklace.''

"Or thinking that the collection has some cash value,'' Althea added. "If you read the article in the paper, you might think it did. Especially the crown. The way O'Meara wrote it—she should go get a job on the *National Enquirer*, the way she writes.''

''What about her?'' Phineas asked. ''No, listen. If there's a big story and she gets to cover it, her career will profit. Or, what if they're about to fire her, and she knows it, she might steal something from the collection so she'd be too important to fire. Because she's the reporter on the story.'' He could really get into this.

''You can write that down if you want to, but that's like writing down Ken because he wants the necklace—and lied to us about it being there, to convince us it wasn't.''

''Why would he do that?'' That was a possibility. Anything was possible.

''I don't know, for the money, maybe he wants money.''

''He has money, they do—he said, remember? Or anyway hinted, about how much she makes?''

''Maybe she keeps it herself? Unless he gambles or something, or has another woman or . . . can we find any of this out?'' Phineas was busy writing. ''Is there any way to find out if O'Meara's about to be fired, or if Ken needs money?''

Althea's mind ran along a different track. ''What about Mrs. Prynn? She's afraid Old Felix will get ahead of dear Olivia in the donation race.''

''Or that Mr. Fletcher, with the same reason, only the other way around. I can't imagine it, but then I'm not a grown-up so I can't imagine what they might get up to.''

Althea grinned. ''This is getting crazy, Fin.''

''I don't mind. I think we have to put down Mrs. Batchelor too.''

''Why her?''

"Because she was so angry, that first day, remember? It didn't make sense, and it still doesn't—Why should she be so angry?" Phineas answered his own question. "Maybe she wants to protect her library, keep it pure, just books. Or keep absolute control over it?" Phineas suggested. "Or preserve the architecture?"

"It's ugly," Althea said.

"She might not think so." Phineas couldn't imagine what someone like Mrs. Batchelor would care so much about that she'd do something weird to get what she wanted. He couldn't imagine an adult caring that much—so that, in a way, he could imagine almost anything, even Mrs. Batchelor sneaking around at night to steal the collection.

"But there's her husband. Maybe she hopes if the college loses the collection her husband's museum will get it. Maybe"—Althea reached across to grab Phineas by the wrist, her eyes sort of glittering and not even stopping to think over her newest idea—"Listen, Fin, maybe we've got it backward. Maybe we've got it all wrong. Who says anyone really intended to succeed, to break into the room and take something out. It could be that someone just wanted to show that a break-in *could* occur."

"Why?" he asked, but what he was thinking was that his sister really *was* smart, was seriously smart.

"To make Dad look bad. It does make him look bad."

"So the collection would be taken away from him? And go to someone else? Who would want it? Or maybe it would go to some*where* else? From the college too. Where would it go?" It made sense to Phineas, this new idea of Althea's.

"To the MFA in Boston, which is where Mr. Van-

81

demark said the family wants it to be. He did say that, didn't he?''

"Or to the museum here. Mr. Batchelor said they didn't have room, but that—or, the valuable pieces at least might go there. But, Althea, you'd have to be a little crazy to go to those lengths—doing something criminal—just because you wanted a certain museum to have something. Or a certain man not to have it. Or a certain place not to. Mrs. Batchelor is weird, but is she crazy enough to do something criminal just to show that something criminal can be done?''

"She's a better candidate than Mr. Vandemark.''

"I don't know about that. Someone who's used to getting his own way, like a dictator, like Noriega. If people like that are crossed, they don't take it lightly.''

Once he'd started thinking suspiciously, Phineas couldn't stop himself. He looked at his sister, and wondered how far she would go to get their parents back together. It took a minute for it to sink in that Althea was looking at him in the same wondering way.

Or how far his father might go, he wondered, not meeting Althea's eyes.

❋ 9 ❋

By the time Phineas came down to the kitchen the next morning, Althea was already there, already dressed, reading, ignoring him. He poured himself a bowl of cereal, topped it generously with sugar, and doused it with milk. He ate standing up, staring into the glass-fronted shelves that held plates and glasses. He knew what his mother would have to say about those shelves: Glass might let you see in, but glass had to be kept clean. Give her Formica cupboards, preferably white, so you could see the dirt right away, and get it.

Phineas poured himself a glass of juice, put two pieces of bread into the toaster, and sat down at the table.

Althea continued to ignore him. She was writing chicken scratches on a piece of paper, her india ink eyebrows gathered together in concentration. "How come you're working down here?" he asked.

She answered without looking up. "In case the phone rings. Dad didn't get back until almost dawn. Not everybody can sleep like the dead."

"Yeah, well, maybe if you turned off the light you'd sleep better," he said, before he thought to stop himself. He was sorry he'd said it even before he saw the combination of anger, and fear, cross her face to settle in her eyes. His parents had at first told him, and then when he was older explained to him, that you had to be considerate of someone's genuine fear. Althea was afraid of the dark, not crazy afraid but seriously afraid. Phineas knew it was as much of a pain for her as the rest of them, maybe even more of a pain. "Sorry," he mumbled.

Althea settled into anger, and stayed there. She ignored him and glowered at him, both at the same time.

"So, were there any phone calls?" he asked.

Althea shook her head.

"What're you doing?" he asked.

She looked up at him, sarcastic under a raised eyebrow, and didn't bother answering. Of course he knew it was Greek. He was just trying to be friendly. He buttered his slices of toast and didn't say anything else.

There was a knock at the front door, *rap rap rap*. Before Phineas could even start to get up, it came again, louder. Althea took off to answer it. Phineas spread peanut butter on his second slice of toast, and wished he'd thought of it sooner so the peanut butter would have been melted by the heat. He put another slice of bread into the toaster so he could have a perfect piece of peanut butter toast.

Two voices at the door, one loud and inquiring—he recognized it, and as it came toward the kitchen he identified it: O'Meara. Althea's voice was low, sort of a murmur, but O'Meara didn't take the hint. "If you don't have coffee, then I'll take a cup of tea, if you have it," she was saying. She came in and plumped herself down on a chair. "When do you think he'll wake up?" she asked, looking over her shoulder at Althea. Then she bent down to pull a notebook and pen out of her bag. That morning she wore a black T-shirt over her jeans, and a jean jacket over the T-shirt.

Althea caught Phineas's eye, and they shrugged at one another. "Do you want regular or herbal tea?" Althea asked.

"Regular. You never know what's in that herbal stuff. Morning, Phineas," O'Meara said.

"Hi." Phineas finished spreading peanut butter over the hot buttered toast. O'Meara looked at it, as if she wished he'd offer her some, and he didn't.

"Dad might sleep until afternoon," Althea said.

"The thing is, I need to talk with him," O'Meara said.

Phineas didn't say anything, and neither did Althea.

"Because of the robbery last night," she said.

Nobody answered her.

"Do you kids know about it?"

"Lemon? Sugar?" Althea asked.

"Milk," O'Meara said, "and sugar. Come on, kids, do you know anything or not? What was taken? Anybody injured? Will the college lose the collection? All I saw was the paragraph this morning in the paper—This is *my* story."

Althea put a mug down in front of her, and a spoon, and the milk carton, and the sugar bowl.

"You must know something," O'Meara said.

After a long wait, Althea said, "Nothing was taken, nothing was damaged."

"Is that the truth? What did happen? Did somebody catch him in the act? Or her, we shouldn't be sexist."

"He was frightened off," Althea said.

O'Meara put down the mug and picked up her pen. "How?"

Althea hesitated.

Phineas chewed slowly. In the first place, he planned to let Althea make the decisions. She was older and she was smarter. In the second place, he was enjoying the melty peanut taste that was coating the inside of his mouth.

"Listen, O'Meara," Althea began, and it sounded as

if she was about to apologize. "It could be that your article is the reason there was a break-in. You didn't exactly tell the precise truth."

It might sound apologetic but it was actually an accusation. O'Meara didn't see it that way. "Pretty good writing, wasn't it?"

"So I don't want to say anything to you now," Althea said.

"I bet you don't know anything." O'Meara drank some tea. "When's your father going to be up do you think?"

Althea shrugged.

O'Meara drank.

Phineas licked peanut butter off his fingers.

"The police report won't be available until this afternoon," O'Meara said. "Dr. Simard told me he's packing, going abroad for a month—and he wasn't on the spot, anyway, nobody called him. He sounded sort of miffed about that. I could go to his house, I suppose." She looked at them. "But it's outside of town."

Phineas got up to pour himself a glass of milk.

"What're you reading?" O'Meara asked. "What is that?" She closed the book to look at the cover. "Greek? What're you doing studying Greek? And during the summer? Killing time," she answered herself. "You ought to look into computer sciences, if studying is your thing. You ought to think about earning a living." She looked down at her notebook and read the little she'd written there. "Althea?"

"Yes?" Warily.

"What frightened him off?" O'Meara was perking up again. "What happened to scare him off?"

Althea shrugged, to say she had no idea and couldn't care less.

Phineas could have warned her. He had a pretty good idea what was going on in O'Meara's mind.

"Then how do you know he was scared? There must be some reason to think so. Do you two kids know anything about the curse of Tutankhamen? For instance," she leaned forward, "when they flew that exhibit around, a few years ago, remember?"

Althea nodded cautiously.

"It went from Egypt to England, first, for a special exhibit, fifty years after it was first found. Do you know that of the crew on that plane, the one that took it from Egypt to London, within a few years, two of the four of the crew members had unexpected disasters happen? One man kicked the mummy's coffin, and later he broke that exact same leg. Another of them was divorced, when he'd been happily married before. And they all said, all the crew, they made jokes about the curse, during the flight. That's why he kicked the coffin. Two more of them had heart attacks. Every one of them, and their families agree, have no doubt about there being something supernatural at work. The pharaoh's curse." She let those words sink in. "What do you think of that?"

"Our mummy's not a pharaoh," Phineas pointed out.

"Then, what scared the burglar off?"

The *blatt* of the telephone broke their uncomfortable silence. Althea went to answer it. Phineas decided to have his say. "You ought to stop hinting at things you don't know anything about. Just to get a story out of them."

O'Meara smiled, and put her notebook back in her bag. "A free press is the backbone of a free nation," she announced. Phineas was trying to think of a question that would tell him if O'Meara was about to be fired. O'Meara kept talking, which interfered with his thinking. "I've got a career investment in a free press. A good reporter follows the story. I'll be back," she said and was gone before he could stop her to ask "How's your job?"

Phineas got to work washing his dishes and setting them on the rack to dry. Althea interrupted to call him to the phone. "That was Mr. Vandemark. He's pretty upset, and he's coming up to talk to Dad. Casey wants to talk to you." She looked worried. "I guess I better make a pot of coffee, and wake Dad up. Do you think?"

"Sure." Phineas didn't know why she was so worried. It wasn't as if their father was the criminal. He went to get the phone. Unless Althea thought he was?

"Phineas?" Phineas waited. "It's me, Casey. Vandemark. Are you free this afternoon?"

"I'm free every afternoon."

"Because my father's coming up, and I was thinking, I could come with him? And we might do something? You wanna? Play tennis, or Monopoly? Unless, do you play chess?"

"No. Althea does."

There was a silence. Phineas waited.

"I was going to ask if you could come down, but now . . ." His voice drifted off. "Anyway, should I?"

"Sure, why not?" Phineas asked. He had hung up before he thought of some reasons why not: If Casey was there, he couldn't hear whatever it was Mr. Vandemark wanted to say to his father, and he wouldn't go with them to see the collection and see the police in action. On the other hand, it would make a change to hang around with someone his own age. He wondered what kind of tennis player Casey was. The kind who always wore whites was his guess.

Whites it was, and whites so white they looked brand new, as if they had never been sweated in. The sneakers that completed the outfit shone white, like snow under sunlight. Phineas was wearing an old pair of baggy outback shorts—so called because they had pockets into which you could stuff everything you might need for survival: dried food, your camping knife, a compass, or, in Phineas's case, tennis balls. He preferred not to wear socks, so he didn't. He had chosen his Billy and the Boingers T-shirt.

Casey stood staring up at Phineas. Phineas could about tell what Casey was thinking. Phineas looked like a hot-dogger. He knew it, and he knew Casey was due for a surprise. "Let's go," Phineas said, and jumped down over all three steps.

Two hours and three sets later, both of them were lying under the shade of a tree, both of them sweaty and red-faced. They were resting up before walking back to the college, halfheartedly watching other games being played. "You're pretty good," Casey said.

"I'm okay. You're not so bad yourself," Phineas answered. He'd taken each set, but none of them easily, and each one with more difficulty than the one before. Casey kept getting there, getting shots back, *plunk, plunk, plunk*.

"I've taken lessons," Casey said.

"So've I."

Casey sat up. "I'd better be getting back," he said, stuffy, or maybe shy. Phineas didn't know.

As they stood up and bent over to get their rackets, Phineas thought to himself how good it felt to really use his muscles, to have sweat drying on him. He'd forgotten how good it felt to be played out. To be a kid, with another kid. The only other times he'd felt like a kid recently were when he was having a good fight with Althea. He didn't want the feeling to end.

"Let's go make some lemonade. We've got lots in the freezer. Unless, do you think your father is waiting for you?"

"No, he was going back, he wasn't planning to stay long. He said he was just going to burn a few ears off. He's going to send George back to pick me up."

"George?" They were walking side by side, both swinging rackets. People coming toward them gave them a wide berth, as if two boys walking back from a tennis game might be dangerous.

"George drives."

Phineas stopped dead. "You mean you've got a chauffeur?"

"A driver," Casey said, the same way he plunked back a forehand.

Phineas let the subject drop. He guessed being rich was something Casey didn't talk about. They got moving again. "Your father isn't going to give my father grief, is he? Because it wasn't my father's fault."

"My father's thinking of hiring a private detective."

"What for?"

"To find out who did it. Or, precisely, who tried to do it."

Phineas burst out laughing. "You're kidding. Is he really? An actual detective?"

After a few steps, Casey laughed too. "It is pretty excessive, isn't it?"

"Seriously excessive," Phineas said.

They were still laughing as they entered the empty house. Phineas took frozen lemonade down, opened it, and put it in the blender with some water. They'd dilute it to taste after it had been, literally, whipped into drinkable shape. Or, precisely, cut, cut into drinkable shape.

Casey sat and watched, accustomed to not doing things himself. "My father thinks that if he can prove the collection is in jeopardy, they can say the terms of the will haven't been met. You know, it's not the money they care about. They care about the name. They want the Vandemark name on a label in the museum."

"The Boston Museum," Phineas said.

"Of course. What other museum is there?"

Phineas didn't know if Casey was being sarcastic or not; he gave him the benefit of the doubt. "That's pretty rotten for my father."

"I know. Mine's pretty selfish. They are. They don't think anyone but them knows how to take care of things. They also don't like letting things go."

Phineas poured out glasses of lemonade, thought about what Casey thought of his family, and didn't answer.

"And it's not even very valuable, it's not like there was anything special in the collection," Casey said.

"There's the mummy."

"Lots of places have mummies. It's not even really old, for a mummy."

"She. Not it, she. I know she's not a pharaoh, or a queen, but—if you saw her, you'd know what I mean."

"I'd like to. Can I?"

Phineas didn't know if he was allowed to show someone the collection, so he avoided Casey's question. "Today? I doubt it. They'll all be . . ."

"Yeah," Casey said. "Doing their important stuff."

He knew exactly what Casey meant. "It's weird, when you see it. Her. It's kind of creepy but mostly . . . old. Hundreds and hundreds of years old, but with the portrait you know what she looked like. Like she's alive.''

"I don't like to think about somebody digging up my body hundreds of years from now," Casey said. "To put it in a museum."

"Why would anyone do that? You're not that important, are you?"

"I don't think so, but they do. One of the things they fight about is whose family is more important. I think they'd get divorced, except they can't."

"Because Vandemarks don't," Phineas guessed.

"Yeah. But they don't spend much time together, and when they're having a big fight my mother doesn't talk to anyone, then she fires a maid or two. Never Mrs. Willis, because good cooks are hard to find. Did your parents fight much?"

Phineas shrugged.

"Don't you ever talk about them?"

"Why should I?"

"Something must be wrong, if she's in Portland, Oregon, and you're here."

"That doesn't mean I should talk about them. Complain."

"How else can you learn how normal your experience is?" Casey asked. "How else can you learn—Phineas, you're stuck with the parents you have, stuck with the life you have, stuck with yourself, stuck. If you don't ever compare."

"Talk to Althea then. She doesn't mind blaming them."

"She doesn't like me."

"That's not true. Or at least, there's nothing personal. She gets nervous around boys. They make her nervous."

"It's interesting—you don't mind talking about Althea. It's just your parents you don't want to talk about."

Phineas had never thought of that. "I guess," he said, thinking of it, "they're making me nervous. More than when they had a fight, because they'd always make up after an hour or so, and then go around for a week, kissing a lot, holding hands, as if they were Romeo and Juliet or something. You know."

Casey shook his head. He didn't know.

"But this wasn't a fight. It was a decision. They talked it over. We all talked it over. It does make me nervous. I guess, I don't feel secure about what they'll do."

"Do you ever feel secure about what grown-ups are doing?" Casey asked.

"No," Phineas said, the word exploding out of him. "They get so complicated, they make everything so complicated. Like, why doesn't your father just let the will stand?"

"Or, why would anyone try to steal the collection?" Casey fell in with Phineas's thinking. "Who would want to?"

"Not kids," Phineas said.

Althea came in through the back door on that remark. "Not kids what?" she asked.

"Unless it was drugs," Phineas said, looking at his sister, who looked just like usual, jeans and sweatshirt, hair in ponytails, dark eyebrows, "kids looking for drug money. The break-in," he told her.

"You watch too much TV," she squelched him. "There are lots of reasons besides drugs why bad things happen."

"There sure are," Casey said.

"Besides," Phineas added, "anyone on drugs would

93

get lost in the cellar. You'd never be able to find your way on drugs.''

''How do you know?'' Althea asked, narrowing her eyes.

''Ease up,'' he told her. ''It was a joke. I wouldn't—''

''You better not,'' she said.

''I wish I had a sister close to my age,'' Casey said.

''No you don't,'' Phineas told him.

''Dad sent me to get you,'' Althea said. ''We're supposed to meet him. Not you, Casey.''

10

THEY LEFT CASEY WAITING FOR GEORGE ON THE front steps. "Where are we going?" Phineas asked. Althea's ponytails bobbed up and down as she hustled along.

"Library."

"Why?"

"The police. Casey's father stirred them up. Don't ask me, Phineas, I'm just doing what I'm told, and Dad told me to get you."

Althea led him up the main steps, through the wooden doors, and into the reading room. A group of people had gathered there, around a big man with a bushy mustache and heavy glasses. Phineas did a double take. The guy looked like he was wearing a Groucho Marx disguise. He wasn't, but just for a second it had looked like he was.

Phineas and Althea brought the number of people up to seven, as they went to stand close behind their father on the thick oriental carpet. Mrs. Batchelor was beside their father, and she watched their entrance, as if they proved her point. Mr. Fletcher was opening a pocket watch he'd taken from his vest pocket, and Ken—dressed scruffy, for Ken, in jeans and deck shoes, his shirttails out, his bearded head looking as if it needed tidying—craned his head around to see the clock, which read 4:35. Phineas decided the big man must be the policeman, because everyone seemed to be waiting for him to give orders. There was nobody else in the reading room, although a few people lingered beyond the door, peering in.

The reading room, with its tables and leather chairs and racks of newspapers and magazines, with its shelves of encyclopedias and the eight long windows, four on each side, could have comfortably held three times as many people without even starting to be full.

"Everybody here?" the Groucho man asked. He didn't wait for an answer. "These the kids?"

"Yes," Mr. Hall said. "Phineas, Althea, this is Detective Arsenault. He wants to ask all of us some questions."

"Except me," Mr. Fletcher said. "I'm here as observer. In my role as attorney to the Vandemark family."

"We know why you're here." Detective Arsenault hesitated, just long enough, before he added, "Sir." He sounded bored, and already tired of them all. His hair was long for a policeman and he wore a jacket and tie, not a uniform. "Mr. Vandemark got the chief's permission for you to be included, I've been told that." And told a couple of other things too, from his tone of voice, although his face looked expressionless. "Now, if I can get on with my job?"

"I'd hope so," Mr. Fletcher answered. "Time is money." He snapped his watch shut and slipped it back into his vest pocket.

They all stood to attention.

"What I want is for you to take a look around, to see if you notice anything different," the detective said. "I've been assigned to this case, and I'm asking you to help me examine the scene of the crime."

"Attempted crime," Mr. Fletcher interrupted.

"Yes, exactly," Detective Arsenault answered. "That is exactly it."

They were looking at each other like opponents over a checkers board, but Phineas couldn't figure out what the game was they were playing.

"Do you mean to imply that until something has been stolen you don't call it a theft?" Ken asked the question, amazed.

"That's only common sense," the detective answered. "Isn't it?"

"You mean," Ken rephrased it, "that unless I actually make off with the goods I'm not guilty? If all I do is want to take them, and plan to take them, and do everything I can to take them but don't succeed?"

"It's only attempted, until you do it. With the crime rate the way it is, attempteds don't get much time in court."

"That's appalling," Ken said. "Don't you think it is?" he asked Mr. Fletcher.

"It's the law," Mr. Fletcher answered.

"But it's wrong," Ken protested.

"Law isn't a moral entity. It's a civic, or social entity. You're an historian, young man, you should appreciate the difference between the two."

"There's always breaking and entering, to charge someone with. There's always attempted," Detective Arsenault said, taking over the conversation again. "If I can proceed?"

Ken subsided, but it was clear he wasn't satisfied. He was shaking his head, paying almost no attention while the detective asked Mrs. Batchelor, "Now, you lock the windows every night?"

"Not me, personally, but yes, the windows are locked every night. I do check every one of them before I close the library."

"Every single one?" He doubted her.

Mrs. Batchelor drew herself up stiff, and pursed her mouth. She didn't deign to answer.

"I'm sorry, ma'am, but this building is three stories high, plus the cellar. There must be I don't know how many windows."

"Forty-eight," Mrs. Batchelor told him. "Of course, the third floor is seldom used, being devoted to storage, and the rare-book room. The cellars, being completely underground, have no windows. If anyone has used the rare-book room, or gone into the storage rooms, he will have asked for the keys from the desk, so those windows aren't part of my daily round. If I didn't make my rounds each evening, I would be failing to take proper precautions. The library is, after all, my responsibility. I am ultimately the one responsible."

Phineas wondered how she could say that. Had she forgotten that the crime, the attempted crime, had taken place in her library?

"I take it then that you will have checked the windows in this room last night?"

"You may take it thus."

"And you can swear that this window was locked." He pointed without drama to the window in question.

Phineas watched Mrs. Batchelor's face, waiting for her to snap out the answer. But she didn't. The pride that had puffed her up left her, like air from a balloon. "I believe it was," she said, slowly and carefully. "I assume it was. But swear? I can't remember checking this window specifically, although I can swear that it is my habit to check each window. I am confident that I would have known if it was unlocked, but I can't swear that I remember checking this particular window, and finding it locked. If you see what I mean."

98

The detective nodded his head, as if what he'd suspected had just been shown to be true.

"Something which is a daily habit," Mrs. Batchelor began, but she dropped the sentence without finishing it.

"We have to assume," the detective said, "that for some reason this window was unlocked. And the thief discovered it, and entered through it. Unless he had a key to the library?"

"But if he had a key," Ken asked, "why would he break through the lock on the door to the cellar? The same key fits both locks."

"Yes, that's the question," the detective agreed. Ken looked pleased with himself, and his question. Phineas was a little disappointed with this detective. He didn't seem to know any more than anyone else.

"Now, Mrs. Batchelor," the detective said, turning back to the thin woman, "are you sure the real objective wasn't the rare-book room? Is there anything in the rare-book room a thief might go after?"

Mrs. Batchelor started nodding before he'd even finished his question. "I'm glad you have some understanding of what treasures a library might hold. We do have an edition of Blake's *Songs of Innocence* and *Songs of Experience*, very rare, very valuable. Because of the illustrations, each of which were done by hand, by the poet himself—"

The detective moved his hand impatiently and she caught herself.

"It's the first place I looked, of course, when I heard the building had been broken into. The Blake is priceless. We'd never be able to afford to replace it. But that room hadn't been discovered, I'm glad to say. I could see no signs that anyone had been in there. Or tried to break in."

"We can assume then that the thief didn't know about it," the detective said, "just as we have to assume that, contrary to the usual practice, the window was left unlocked. Shall we move along?"

The group followed him to gather around the door that opened from the library's main floor to the staircase into the cellars. "Does anyone notice anything odd here?" the detective asked. He waited, while everyone stared at the door.

"I take it you mean beyond the obvious," Mr. Fletcher said.

The obvious was just what they would see again downstairs: the results of a crowbar inserted between the door and the frame, and then levered back until wood split, forcing the metal plate backward into the splintered wood until it was possible—using the crowbar as a bat if appearances didn't lie—to force the door open.

Nobody saw anything to comment on. Phineas thought that the thief must have been pretty strong, even with a crowbar, but he didn't trust his thinking. He knew enough about levers, which he'd studied in fifth-grade science, to know that he couldn't remember by how much a lever multiplied force. The detective would surely know that, so Phineas kept quiet. They all trooped down the staircase, then turned left down a corridor, left again, left once more, and then right—following Mrs. Batchelor's lead—until they stood before the door to room 015.

Nobody had anything to observe, so they entered the room. The detective told them what he wanted. "I know you reported nothing missing, Mr. Hall, but I just want you—all of you who worked to set out the collection, and anyone who's seen it as it originally was—I want you to look carefully around. You probably won't see anything, but . . .'' He turned around to look over the room. "That's the mummy?" he asked, his voice changed for the question. He walked over to look down at the wrapped figure. "It's . . . really something, isn't it? I never—well.'' He drew himself up. "Look around, don't touch anything, just see if anything at all is different. Even just shifted on its shelf.''

Phineas lagged by the doorway. He'd be no help, anyway. He didn't know why he'd been asked along. If this was what detective work was like, it was pretty boring.

The detective and Mr. Fletcher also stood back. Mrs. Batchelor did go into the room, but mostly she stood aside and pretended to be looking, pretended that she was important to what was going on. She looked worried; that was what Phineas thought. He wondered if she had some suspicion. If she did, why wouldn't she speak up? It was her library, after all. Then he wondered if the look on her face was guilt, not worry.

The detective stood with his hands in his pockets. He didn't take notes, he didn't ask questions, he just watched. If it were a Disney movie, Phineas thought, the detective would be whistling, to distract attention from his watching.

Althea stayed by the mummy, letting her father and Ken check the shelves. The room was silent, with the thick silence of a class taking a test everybody wanted to do well on, and thought they had a chance to do well on. The air control machinery hummed.

Phineas was getting a little restless. He didn't know how long they were going to have to stay there before the detective dismissed them. He went to stand beside Althea, which meant standing at the mummy's feet.

She was small, lying down, wrapped stiff in strips of cloth, her feet pointed at the ceiling. Small, and sad. Phineas had the odd, angry idea that she should have

101

been left alone, left where she was found, left buried in her own country, in her own time. But he guessed you couldn't blame people—historians, scientists—for always wanting to find out more. That was their job. It was their nature too, to want to take things away, into their own labs in their own countries, and take them apart, and find out answers.

His father turned around and looked at Ken, with his eyebrows raised in questioning. Ken shook his bearded head. Nothing missing, nothing wrong.

"Nothing," Mr. Hall said to the detective.

"I was afraid of that," the detective answered. "Well, that's that. Nothing more I can do. It looks like a dead end, Mr. Fletcher. That's what my report will say."

"It's the crown, of course," Ken said.

"Crown?" the detective asked, politely.

Ken didn't notice the detective's lack of interest. "There's a funerary crown," he said. He reached around and took it off its place on the shelf, his hands more gentle than his appearance would suggest. He held it out. "It's in perfect condition," Ken said, "and beautiful craftsmanship. I can't say exactly what a museum might pay for it. A lot."

Detective Arsenault went over to look more closely. "What is it, gold?"

"Gilded bronze." Ken turned around to put the wreath back on the shelf. "It worries me, Sam."

Detective Arsenault didn't give Mr. Hall a chance to speak. "You think that's what the thief was after?"

"How would I know?" Ken asked. "But if I were a thief, it's what I'd take."

"You'd have to know your stuff, though, wouldn't you? To know its value," the detective pointed out.

"If I were a thief, I'd make a point of knowing my stuff," Ken announced.

Nobody said anything for a while. They were all waiting to be told what to do next, except for Detective Arsenault, who must have been wondering what he should tell them to do next, or so Phineas thought. "Place is like a tomb," the detective said.

"Mr. Hall?" Mrs. Batchelor had finally made up her mind to speak. She cleared her throat. "If you would prefer, my husband was sincere in his offer to have the crown stored at the museum."

Althea looked at Phineas, and he thought he knew what she was thinking. "I might take him up on that," their father said.

"My husband is at the museum until seven on Wednesdays, because the museum is open Wednesday evenings until seven. You could call him now, from my office, and I'm reasonably confident that the crown could be taken into safekeeping tonight."

"That sure would take a load off my mind, Sam," Ken added, as if Mr. Hall was hesitating. "In fact, why don't I stick around to ride shotgun when we move it. My car's out back."

"Then I'll be the one riding shotgun," Mr. Hall pointed out. "Detective Arsenault, is there any objection to moving it? Always assuming the museum will accept it."

"I don't think you need worry about that," Mrs. Batchelor said.

"I see no difficulty," the detective answered. "Although my hunch is that it's the mummy he was after. Since he could have grabbed that crown and been gone, even with the alarm going. But I'll be the first to admit I'm no expert," he said, with a nod at Ken.

"Besides, we're taking the mummy off first thing in

the morning, for X rays,'' Phineas's father said. "And as soon as you give the okay, which I hope will be immediately, they're ready to put a new door on here, with a new lock, to which only the captain of the security guards and I will have keys. No insult intended, Ken.''

"None taken,'' Ken said. "I'm going to be leaving the country so soon, it would be silly to be given the new key.''

"And the alarm's still in place?'' Detective Arsenault asked.

Mr. Hall nodded.

"I think you've done everything you can. I don't think there's any danger of a repeat visit. I figure, it was probably kids. It's summer,'' he said glumly, "kids get bored, they read the paper too. But at least your thief wasn't a professional, which is what would worry me, speaking personally.''

"How do you know he wasn't?'' Mr. Fletcher asked.

"Well, sir, in the first place, he wouldn't have jimmied the doors. He'd have had a set of skeleton keys. Secondly, he'd have spotted the alarm, and turned it off. But mostly, a professional would have succeeded.''

❈ 11 ❈

It was eight o'clock before Althea and their father got home, with Ken Simard tagging along behind them. Phineas took one look at his father and got three cans of chicken noodle soup out of the cupboard. He turned on the oven to four hundred degrees, and started buttering the tops of saltines while the soup heated. They were all too wiped out to say anything and Phineas was too busy to talk—putting the cookie pan of buttered crackers into the stove, setting the table—

"Ken, will you be staying for supper?" he asked. "It's just canned soup and crackers." Sometimes, with guests who wouldn't go away, you had to make your hints pretty loud and clear.

"Gee, you know? I'd like to. If it's not too much trouble. If there's enough for me. If you don't mind, Sam?"

It was lucky he didn't ask Althea if *she* minded. Phineas grinned into the simmering soup, pale yellow with chunks of chicken and streaks of noodle.

"Won't your wife be expecting you?" Mr. Hall asked. Phineas wondered if that was the grown-up version of a hint. If it was, Ken missed it entirely.

"Michelle's in Boston, looking into a company that might be a good subject for a takeover bid. She's got a full week scheduled, which means she won't be here to see me off on my great adventure. However, that's the way it is, if we're married to successful women with careers of their own, isn't it?''

Phineas set out four soup bowls, four spoons, four glasses. He was doing what his mother would have done. He didn't mind that. Then he asked, as his mother would have, ''Do you want a beer?''

Both men did.

Phineas opened two cans and poured them into glasses. It wasn't so bad, being a housewife. He had come back to an empty house, watched a rerun of ''Magnum,'' then a rerun of the ''Cosby Show,'' then a rerun of ''Newhart,'' and now they were all thanking him for making dinner. Ken was more grateful than the others.

''Really good, Phineas,'' he said, as if Phineas had done anything more than open three cans and add water. ''I for one will sleep better, knowing the crown is safe. I know, I know,'' he raised a hand as if Mr. Hall were about to say something, which he clearly wasn't since he was spooning soup into his mouth as fast as he could, ''it's your concern, not mine. I admit to feeling—not exactly proprietary, but perhaps the analogy is to a groom in an arranged marriage, waiting for his affianced to grow up? I've had a couple of ideas for the paper, but what I'd really like to try is''—he pushed the half-empty soup bowl away and leaned forward on his elbows—''something for a more popular market. Maybe the magazine section of the *Times*? Or the *Atlantic*, *Harper's*, something in that class. To explain the beauty of the thing, the craftsmanship, the symbolism of its use. It could be a crossover paper. So I'm in the happy position of having something to go away for, and something to come back to.''

''What is it that's waiting for you in England, Ken?''

Mr. Hall asked. He took some crackers. "Anyone else want peanut butter with these?"

"Waiting for certain? Nothing, of course. Nothing's certain until you hold it in your hand, is it? But at the Bodleian, anything might turn up. They have wonderful materials, and with all the bequests over the centuries, they have so much that they haven't cataloged everything they have. You can never tell what might turn up—especially among the papers of those nineteenth-century explorers and travelers, who bought up whatever. If I let my imagination go unreined, I dream of Platonic dialogue, or an unknown Aristophanes. Imagine the fallout from something like that, Althea. I heard of a man who discovered a Marlowe manuscript nobody knew about, at the Bodleian, this was in the twenties, not all that long ago. Sometimes, recently, I've felt that my fortunes are about to change."

"For the better, I assume," Mr. Hall said, trying to lighten things up.

But Ken couldn't be distracted. "I'm not the only one to hope for Harvard, am I? A scholar wouldn't feel like a fish out of water the minute he stepped off campus there. That's how I feel here, off campus, especially out where we live—like a very small fish out of a very small pond. At Harvard—everyone knows the scholars, and admires them. Well, as always, I'm talking too much. I've got a busy night, big day tomorrow, lift-off time is three o'clock for the shuttle to New York. I guess I ought to be on my way. Thanks for the supper. Thanks also for setting my mind at ease about the crown. I don't know what that vulture lawyer's hidden agenda is, whatever the family puts him up to, but I bet that you got in its way tonight."

"For that, you owe me," Phineas's father said.

Ken looked surprised, alarmed.

"It's been a horrible evening," Mr. Hall explained. "First all that waiting around, to get the new door hung, and a lock in, then for Mark Batchelor to make his appearance with the papers for me to sign." By then, Ken realized that Mr. Hall was half joking, exaggerating everything. "Pelting across Portland—Althea in the backseat with the crown on her lap, me getting nervous every time we stopped for a light—And then Mark Batchelor making the process at the museum vault as slow as a coronation. . . ."

Both men stood up. "I don't think he delayed on purpose," Ken said. "Why would he? But as Lucille will tell you, if you're ever foolish enough to get her started, as a curator he is a guardian of Art. Capital A, Art. Capital G, guardian too. You weren't surprised at all the paperwork, were you? You don't think . . . ?"

"Think what?"

"Nothing. Nothing. I didn't mean anything. Although I personally thought Lucille was looking just a little too pleased. Didn't you?"

"Frankly, I'm too tired to notice anything or anyone. Even to take offense."

When Mr. Hall returned to the kitchen and sank into his chair, Althea greeted him. "Ken's tedious, isn't he?"

"Seriously wimpy," Phineas corrected her.

"Unlike your father, with his boyish charm," Mr. Hall reminded them. "Your father who has never uttered a boring word. Who is a macho model for both of you."

"Okay," Althea said. "It was snide. But what got him going tonight? He was unusually verbose, you have to admit that, Dad."

"I admit," Mr. Hall said. "I apologize. I didn't think he'd stay for dinner."

"I think he likes being where the excitement is," Althea said, and yawned. "You can go with Dad tomorrow morning, Fin, for the X ray. I'm going to sleep in, and wake up when I feel like it, and get some work done."

"That sounds all right." Phineas had never ridden in an ambulance.

"We have to meet them at six," his father warned him. "At the parking lot entrance."

Althea smirked. "I put my hours in today, while you were probably vegged out in front of the TV."

"It's okay, nobody has to come with me. You don't have to, Phineas."

"But I want to," Phineas said, which was mostly true.

So there he was at 6:00 A.M., standing in chilly damp air that was barely light although the sun was long risen. "One misty, moisty morning," his father recited, and drank from the mug of coffee he'd carried with him. Phineas hadn't brought anything to eat or drink and he was already sorry.

"Have I got time to run home and get something to eat?" he asked.

"Not if they're on time. Stick with me, son. I'll take you out for breakfast while they're doing the X rays."

"Nothing will be open."

"There'll be a cafeteria at the hospital."

"I'm starving."

"No you're not. Very hungry, maybe, but nowhere near starving. Listen, I bet that's them now." He drained the mug and jammed it into the pocket of his yellow rain jacket.

The square shape of the ambulance emerged from the drizzly fog, its headlights glowing. It pulled up beside them and a man climbed down from the passenger seat. He went to open the rear door. A young woman got out from behind the wheel. She was long-legged and her red hair was cut to brush back short from the sides of her face but left hanging long down her back. She wore jeans, and a jeans jacket. Her mouth worked steadily at a wad of gum. She looked bored. "You Samuel Hall?" she asked and when Mr. Hall said yes she said, "Okay, where's this body at?"

"It's a mummy, actually," Mr. Hall said.

"I know that."

Phineas and his father led the way, while the two attendants came behind, wheeling the stretcher. The cellar lights turned on automatically at 5:30, so the hallways were brightly lit. The bare cement walls looked as cold as they felt. Phineas rubbed at his arms. White cinder block walls and blank doors, with numbers painted beside them—that was all there was to see. The wheels on the stretcher had a rattle-and-hum sound that echoed in the empty hallways. Their four sets of sneakers made soft, unechoing sounds. They stopped in front of room 015.

The door was open. Except for the light from the hallway, the room within lay dark.

"What—?" Mr. Hall said, and flicked on the light switch.

The mummy was gone. All that was left was the shroud she'd been lying on, like an old sheet left on the table, an old dirty sheet.

Phineas went up to the table. He thought, somehow, that if he got closer he would see the mummy, even though it was obvious that she wasn't there.

"Dammit," his father said, in a low choked growl. "Damn and blast, and—"

110

The young woman came to stand beside them. "You been ripped off, mister," she said.

"I don't understand," Mr. Hall said.

"To the tune of one body," she said.

"Not a body, a mummy," he corrected her.

"Same thing," she said, cracking her gum.

"Not the same thing at all," Mr. Hall said, almost yelling.

"Looks like someone went through this door with a blowtorch," the male attendant announced from behind them.

Phineas didn't care. He didn't know what to think. He couldn't think. He looked around the long room, hoping to see the mummy lying on the floor, looking up at the ceiling with her little smile. She wasn't there, and he wasn't surprised, but he kept feeling that if he just looked harder he'd see her.

"Nothing for us here," the young woman said. "We better get on back to where we might be needed."

Phineas's father nodded his head. The ambulance attendants left the room, with the sound of stretcher wheels.

"I'll have to call the police, Phineas," his father said, and now he sounded tired out. "And Mr. Vandemark. A plague on both your houses," he said, and he slammed a fist onto the empty table. "A plague on everyone's house!"

"Hey," asked the woman's voice from the hall. "Can someone show us the way out?"

That was something Phineas could do. "I'll do it, Dad," he said. "I'm really sorry."

"It's not your fault," his father answered, still without looking up from the empty sheet. His voice was low again, dull.

"I know that, but—anyway, I'll be right back."

111

"And Dan Lewis too." His father went right on talking, as if Phineas, already at the door, was still standing beside him. "Lucille, President Blight . . . But I don't understand, what happened to the alarm?"

❊ 12 ❊

"THE MUMMY'S GONE."

Althea looked up from her bowl of cereal, the spoon halfway to her mouth. Their father had stopped at the phone in the hall and was dialing it, then talking into it.

"What do you mean, gone?"

"Gone, you know, like, gone. Not there. Stolen, missing, lost—don't be stupid, Althea."

Her eyebrows drew together. "What's going on?" she asked, which was just what his father had asked.

"They cut through the door with a blowtorch, or that's what we think. That's what it looked like.

"It doesn't make sense, Fin."

"All that was left was the shroud."

The more he said, the worse Phineas felt. He didn't know why he should feel so bad over a mummy. He didn't know why that mental picture of the table, empty, just the shroud lying there like someone's tossed-away towel, should make him feel so bad.

"We haven't had any breakfast, or anything to eat," he said. He opened the refrigerator, took out eggs and English muffins. His father would need a good breakfast, after what had happened, before the day that awaited him. "I guess these were professionals after all," Phineas announced.

"I don't understand," Althea said. She got up from the table and stood beside him while he cracked eggs into a bowl. She didn't do anything, she just stood there, watching him.

"What's so hard to understand?" Phineas turned to look at his sister, their eyes level. "The mummy's been stolen. It's gone. Probably forever."

"I thought it was the crown that was valuable."

"Apparently not." For a minute, he thought he was going to get angry at Althea. She kept making him say it over and over. He whisked the eggs with a fork. The mummy was hundreds of years old, so he didn't know why it should bother him so much.

"I mean, who would want a mummy? What would you do with it?"

"Don't you even care?" Phineas demanded, turning on her, never mind that the fork was dripping raw egg down onto the floor.

"Of course." But she didn't sound upset. "I care about Dad, especially. He'll lose the collection."

"But it's not his fault."

"But he's in charge, he's the one responsible. They'll blame him." She stared at Phineas without seeing him. "Who would want a mummy? Seriously, Fin, who? Unless she was buried with that necklace, so it's simple stealing, and then it could be anyone. Who else but museums wants mummies?"

Phineas put the split muffins into the toaster and pushed the lever down. Butter bubbled in the frying pan on the stove. He had no idea. His father's voice spoke into the phone. "Detective Arsenault? I'm sorry to call you so early. It's Sam Hall, at Vandemark—Yes, well, there's bad news. The mummy has apparently been stolen."

Phineas poured eggs into the pan and turned down the heat. You had to cook scrambled eggs gently, he

114

remembered his mother saying that; otherwise they got too dry, and leathery.

"Museums, places like schools with collections of their own, people with collections," Althea said, talking to herself. "But none of those would steal, would they? Or, if they did, they'd go after a mummy that was more valuable, from an earlier period. Not ours."

Phineas stirred the eggs, gently. His father hung up the phone, then dialed another number. "Yes, is Mr. Vandemark in," he said. "Samuel Hall, from the college."

"She's not worth anything, not in herself," Althea said.

"Look, Althea, could you set the table and pour some juice?"

"What? Oh, sure. What does Dad say?"

On the phone, Mr. Hall said, "Why should I call him in? He's leaving for England today. He may have already left. It's my responsibility, Mr. Vandemark. My sole responsibility. I accept that. I don't need Ken here to deflect the fire, or justify my decisions."

Phineas buttered the muffins and served eggs onto plates.

"Yes, I can be there at noon. Yes, I imagine I'll be done at the police station by then. Who, Phineas? He's right here. Phineas?"

"Breakfast is on," Phineas told his father, as he took the phone. He didn't know why Mr. Vandemark would want to talk to him.

But it wasn't Mr. Vandemark, it was Casey. "I was going to see if you could come down for the day today, or tomorrow," Casey said. "But I guess it's bad timing. I just want you to know that I wanted to ask you over."

"Yeah," Phineas said. This was something else whoever had stolen the mummy had taken away from him.

"And I don't think I ought to come up today, when my father does," Casey's voice said. "He's pretty angry. He probably wouldn't let me anyway."

"So I'll see you whenever," Phineas said.

"Whenever."

They ate breakfast in silence. Althea just sat and stared into space. Mr. Hall stared at the food he was eating, as if he wasn't seeing it. Phineas stared at the two of them.

"All right," Mr. Hall said when his plate was empty. "I'm going to take a shower before I go to the police station. There's no reason why I shouldn't look clean, and feel clean, is there?"

They both shook their heads at him.

He stood up and looked down at them. "Your mother should be here," he said, and sounded angry about it. He turned abruptly and left the room. They listened to his feet going up the stairs.

"We've got to do something," Althea said, her voice low.

"What should we do? Should we call Mom?"

"That's the last thing I want to do. Sometimes you are really dense, Phineas."

When their father came back downstairs, they hadn't moved from the table, and they hadn't spoken a word. Mr. Hall wore a khaki suit, and a tie. His cheeks glowed from being shaved. His hair had been slicked down by a wet brush. He looked like a businessman about to go to work in an office, except that there was something about his face that could never look like a businessman. Even when he looked troubled, as he did right then, his face looked ready to laugh, if there was anything he could find to laugh at, and his eyes were thoughtful, as if he was ready to think if there was anything to think about.

His children stared at him.

"Your mother would tell me to wear it," he said. "Dressing for power."

"You look good," Phineas said.

"It's only khaki," Mr. Hall said. "I don't know when I'll get back, probably after lunch, I hope before dinner. I don't know what's going to happen."

"You look good," Phineas said again. He didn't know what else to say. He'd never heard his father sound so discouraged before.

After the front door had closed behind him, Althea spoke. "This is serious, Fin."

"I'm going to wash the dishes." Frankly, he didn't want to think about it. He didn't want to have to think about it.

Althea moved beside him, but not to help out with clearing or washing. She just stuck with him to keep her face close to his ear. "What are you going to do?" she demanded.

"Like I said, the dishes."

"No, about it."

"What can I do? Nothing," he answered himself. "We're only kids, Althea." He turned on the water, hoping that might shut her up.

Althea just talked louder, standing so close she was crowding him. "When a married couple each has a career, then neither of them can afford to be a failure," she said.

He shrugged.

"Which has been bothering Dad, all these years."

"He wasn't a failure. He's a good teacher."

"I know that, and you know that, and Mom does, and his students too—but what about everyone else? People don't think very highly of a high-school

117

teacher. If people thought teachers were important, they'd pay them more. Didn't you ever think about that? What it means to be in a low-paying job? Why do you think housewives have so little self-respect?''

"Does everything have to be feminist to you?" Phineas demanded.

Althea barely hesitated. "That's why this job is so important to Dad. College professors are respected, at least people respect them. Mom had to know that."

Phineas took a scouring pad to the frying pan. "It's not as if they're the only married couple who have two jobs."

"Two jobs on two opposite coasts of a large country."

Phineas opened his mouth to let her know what he thought of that dumb argument, but the *blatt-blatt* of the phone cut him off. Althea answered it. Phineas turned off the water to listen.

"No, Mr. Lewis, he isn't, he's down at the police station. And after that, he's going to Mr. Fletcher's office, to meet with Mr. Vandemark. . . . I think it makes him nervous too. . . . Oh, then I'll tell him to pick up the new key. Thanks, Mr. Lewis."

Althea returned to the kitchen. "They've already put in another new door."

Phineas had been thinking: "Two people, you'd need two people. Or, at least, it would be easier with two. Carrying a mummy."

"Who is there two of, except the Batchelors—and I don't know, would he risk his job so she could have her job the way she wants it? Did you get the feeling he was that crazy about her?"

"How can you tell if a husband is crazy about his wife?" Phineas asked.

118

Blatt blatt, the phone answered him. Althea went to get it, and Phineas mopped up the table and counters.

"That woman," Althea muttered, returning.

"O'Meara," Phineas guessed. He didn't know where that guess had come from, but he knew he was going to be right. It was the same feeling that he had when he served up an ace, a sure knowledge that began before he'd even begun to swing his racket down into the follow-through. "What did she want?"

"I hung up on her. She must have one of those short-wave radios, with a police band. Otherwise, how could she have found out so soon?"

"You were rude," Phineas guessed.

Althea shrugged, then smiled, then laughed. "Pretty much. There are two of us, Fin, and two of either of us with Dad."

"Dumb. That's seriously dumb."

"Besides, there wouldn't have to be two. One person alone could carry the mummy."

"Did you think Mrs. Batchelor was looking smug?"

"And O'Meara—if calling us up is a bluff, calling us up and pretending she just found out."

"Why not Ken?"

"If I thought he could smuggle the mummy into England—no, into the sacred Bodleian—I'd go ask him, you can bet on it."

"Or Mr. Vandemark could have hired someone. No, I'm serious. Casey said he was talking about hiring a private detective, after the first time and—"

"Casey was putting you on. He must have been."

"I don't think so. If you can hire someone, doesn't he do what you tell him to?"

Althea considered. "I hope not, because if that's the kind of people Dad's up against, he doesn't have a chance."

"Dad's not so easy to outsmart." But Phineas wasn't convinced.

"Maybe, but if people like that really want to win out—"

Phineas considered that. "Are you saying you think Dad should give up?"

Althea's dark eyebrows rose, impatient. "No, I'm not. I was just thinking. Something you don't know anything about."

Blatt-blatt, the phone said.

Phineas waited.

Althea waited.

Blatt-blatt, the phone said.

Phineas figured he'd better get it, since she was in a stubborn mood.

"I got the last two," she called after him.

Blatt-bla—"Hello?" Phineas said.

Silence. A breathing kind of silence.

"Hello," Phineas said. This was a little creepy.

"I know where she is," somebody whispered.

She? Who she? The questions flashed across Phineas's mind, faster than light. It took no time at all to feel fear. Althea? She was right behind him in the kitchen. His mother?

"You want to know where?" the whisperer asked.

Phineas couldn't think of what to say. He didn't want to know. It could be a wrong number.

"Who—" Who are you calling? he meant to ask, but the whisperer cut him off.

"You know. You know. By the tennis courts."

"What—" What tennis courts? he was going to ask, but there was only a click, and a dial tone.

Phineas's fingers clutched the receiver. "Althea!" he called.

"What? What's wrong?" She was beside him in a second.

He held the phone out to her. She took it, watching his face, listened, looked puzzled and worried, and hung it up. "Fin? Who was it?"

He was trying to see if he remembered what had been said. He was concentrating, to remember it exactly. "I don't know. Somebody who whispered. He said—she said—I don't know if it was a man or a woman, Althea."

"But what did they say? It's okay, Phineas, just relax. Tell me. It's not Dad, is it? Has anything happened to Dad?"

Phineas shook his head and then—feeling as if the memory would fly out of it, like drops of water when he'd been swimming and shook his head—he hurried to say it before he forgot. "He said she was by the tennis courts. He said I knew who." He didn't know why he was so rattled. Except that it was so creepy.

"The tennis courts in the park?" Althea asked.

"I don't know any others." Phineas pictured the courts, a dozen broad open spaces in line, surrounded by a twelve-foot fence. But there were trees and bushes around the courts, so you could hide a mummy there. "Is the ground wet?" he asked. "But why call us, Althea?"

"Did he ask for you by name?" Phineas shook his head. "So he just called the house, or she, because it could have been a woman. Anybody who read O'Meara's article would know who to call. Let's go look for her, Phineas."

"Shouldn't we call the police station and tell Dad?"

"Not until we're sure. Come on, Fin. What if somebody else finds it, someone who doesn't know what it is, or doesn't care, or who just takes it away? What if it gets wet?"

"The fog's already burned off," Phineas said, but he was halfway out the door before he'd finished the sentence, and Althea was on his heels.

❊ 13 ❊

THEY RAN, THEN WALKED WHEN A STITCH IN ALTHEA'S side made it impossible for her to run any longer. "We should have taken our bikes," Phineas muttered.

"We can't—carry her—with bikes," Althea gasped. "Can't you—slow—?"

Phineas turned into the park entrance. He had a little sweat worked up, but he could still have been running. "Wait," Althea gasped from behind him. He turned and waited for her to catch up. "Not—a jock—you know."

Phineas didn't waste his breath on that put-down. What if some kids found the mummy, and messed around with it? Before they got there. If it was the mummy.

They went up the low ridge that overlooked the courts. A few games were in progress, and as many courts were unoccupied. Sunlight poured over everything. Phineas, his feet hurrying down the hill, figured that probably the mummy had been left in the trees and bushes behind the courts.

They saw it almost immediately, a lumpy shape half tucked under a bush. It looked like somebody's garbage. That was because it was in fact concealed in two black trash bags, one pulled up over and one pulled down over, with the plastic drawstring tied in the middle. Althea knelt down beside it.

Phineas let her take charge. She was breathing heavily, but she didn't wait to catch her breath. It didn't look like a mummy to him, but it was definitely body size. Althea's hands went over it, fingers spread wide, as she tried to see by touch.

The reason it didn't look like a mummy was because there was no bump where the feet stood up; but that, Phineas told himself, didn't mean anything, if it was lying on its side, or on its stomach. He watched Althea's face. Althea watched her own hands, her eyebrows a dark line of concentration. Finally she looked up. "I think so." She took a breath. "I think I can feel the portrait. She's all wrapped up—like in a blanket? Something soft. And thick."

"Now what?" Phineas wondered.

"Now we call Dad. No, you stay here. I'll go."

"Why should I stay? You're older."

"Because," Althea said as she got to her feet, "if somebody comes along you'll be able to stop them. People listen to you. Don't argue, you know I'm right, but you always want to argue. Where's a pay phone, Fin, do you know?"

"At the refreshment stand." He pointed. "You can't see it from here, but you will once you get to the top of the hill."

Althea headed off.

"Do you have money?" he called after her.

"Don't need it to call the police," she called back.

Phineas settled down to wait. He didn't settle down beside the mummy—if it was the mummy. He stood leaning against a tree, sort of watching the tennis players—there was one man with an interesting backhand stroke that began not low, but high, at his shoulder, which put a slice on the ball so it bounced low—and sort of wondering. The thief had called their house. If

124

it was the mummy in the garbage bags, then the thief had known to call them. That had to mean something.

And the voice hadn't sounded surprised to be talking to a kid. As if he'd known who Phineas was.

Or maybe he just didn't care who he talked to. That was possible. Maybe anyone who read O'Meara's article in the paper could have figured out from the pictures which one Samuel Hall was, and then spied on them. But wouldn't they have noticed somebody spying on them? And why would anyone spy on them, anyway, since it was the mummy he was interested in? The mummy he was after.

Then why return the mummy?

Anyone connected to the college knew who they were, and where they lived. Anyone who was there when the collection arrived too.

And why did he keep assuming it was a man? A woman could wield a blowtorch. A woman could carry the mummy around. The mummy was more bulky than heavy.

Phineas looked down at the lumpy garbage bags at his feet. The sunlight made the plastic glisten like water. It was about quarter of eleven, he figured. Althea had been gone for maybe four minutes, it would be about ten before she got back, then another ten or fifteen before his father and Detective Arsenault could show up. . . . He didn't know if he should move the mummy out of the sunlight. If it was the mummy. He didn't know what the kind of heat that built up inside a plastic garbage bag would do to a mummy.

Maybe nothing. The reason mummies still existed was because Egypt was such a hot country. But Egypt was a hot, dry country, desert, not tropics, and Maine got a fair amount of rain.

It made Phineas edgy, just standing there, standing

125

still, so he decided to pace back and forth, like a soldier on guard duty, to pace off the time before Althea returned. He wouldn't abandon the bags, just take twenty paces along beside the tennis courts. He counted his steps. Then he turned.

Two policemen were hurrying down the hillside, sideways so they wouldn't lose balance. They were coming for him. Phineas knew that without even wondering how he knew. He went back to stand beside the mummy.

A couple of tennis players stopped playing to watch whatever excitement there would be.

The two police officers, both men, strode toward him, in blue uniforms, guns at their sides, faces shadowed under their hats. Phineas pushed his hair into place with his fingers, as if he were a guilty person trying to look innocent. They made him nervous the way they stared at him and didn't say a word.

One had a mustache and one didn't. Didn't was the spokesman. "You the kid who called?"

Phineas shook his head. "That was my sister. It sure didn't take you long."

The mustached officer smiled, as if he didn't like a joke Phineas had made. "Don't be sarcastic, kid. We're busy men. One hour isn't bad for a nonemergency call."

"I'm not being sarcastic. She just left, about five minutes ago, to call the police."

"That so? Then you're the second call we got on this. Probably somebody's garbage, all the excitement over nothing." The mustached officer bent down to pull the bag off.

"Wait!" Phineas cried. "Don't do that!"

The man ignored him. His fingers gripped plastic.

Phineas crouched down and grabbed his hand. "We think it's the mummy." A hand fell on his shoulder.

Phineas talked, fast. "The one stolen from the college last night. Detective Arsenault's case. Please don't touch it."

They looked at one another and made their decision without a word. "Okay, tell."

Phineas told, concluding, "My father will be here any minute."

"How do we know this isn't some cock-and-bull story?"

Phineas didn't know how they'd know. "It isn't. Honest," he said. "If you'll just wait, you'll see." He thought. "What would be the point of it, to waste your time?"

"Beats me," the officer, who still had a hand on Phineas's shoulder, said. "Ralph?" he asked.

"Can't do any harm," the mustached man said. "If it's a body, it won't get any deader."

They all settled down on the ground around the garbage bags. "Somebody else called you about this?" Phineas asked.

"Some kids said there was this bag, might be a body."

"Who were they?"

"Just some kids playing tennis."

"But they didn't open it," Phineas wondered.

"Hey, kid, if this is a body, I can tell you you don't want to see it. Or smell it. I can promise you that. Thank God for TV, everybody knows you don't touch anything around the scene of a crime. If this *is* a crime and not an illegal garbage drop."

"Even if it's the mummy," Phineas promised them, "there's a crime, because it was stolen."

Sirens sounded in the distance. The sirens stopped and it was only seconds before Phineas saw his father—his frizzy hair no longer slicked down—come sidling down the hill, with the big detective moving parallel to him. Phineas waved. Althea was just coming around the other side of the fenced courts.

"Guess we're not needed," Ralph said. "Back to business. See you around, kid." They were out of earshot before Phineas remembered that he ought to thank them.

By that time, the three Halls and Detective Arsenault all stood around the garbage bags, looking down. It reminded Phineas of a funeral, at least the way movies showed funerals, everybody standing around, looking down at something that had a dead body in it. The detective finally spoke. "Let's see what we've got, shall we?"

"I'd like to wait until the mummy is out of the open, somewhere safe. . . . I'm sorry," Mr. Hall said. "I'm pretty sure I'm overreacting but I'd hate to do it wrong. I'd much rather look like a fool, or inconvenience everyone, than have something else go wrong that I could help. . . . " His voice trickled off, worried.

"But what if it isn't the mummy?" Detective Arsenault asked. "What if it's some other body? Or even somebody's garbage?"

"It felt soft and thick, what I touched," Althea told him. "I felt something very like the portrait. No, Dad," she reassured her father, "I didn't put any pressure on it. But it felt thickly wrapped. Nobody would wrap up garbage like that, would they? What would be the point?"

The detective looked doubtful. He was a busy man, probably. Phineas could see why he wouldn't want to waste his time, if it turned out not to be the mummy.

"The ambulance will be here any minute," Mr. Hall said. "It would be a big favor. . . ."

"I guess I can. I guess this mummy can't be replaced."

"We could probably get another, if it was a mummy that was wanted," Mr. Hall said, carefully precise. "It's not like this is the mummy of any historical personage. The mummy isn't anyone in particular. It's not like it's one of a kind. Except insofar as every individual is one of a kind."

"Like I said," Detective Arsenault said, "irreplaceable."

They were ignoring Phineas and Althea.

"Irreplaceable," Phineas's father agreed.

At that point, the ambulance driver arrived, the same woman with a different young man in tow. "I guess you found your body. We still taking it in for an X ray?"

"Can we?" Mr. Hall asked.

"Why not? X ray's still open. Exactly how fragile is this thing?"

"Assume it's as fragile as spun glass," Mr. Hall said.

"Or a spinal injury. You better let us handle it, then. Stand back—you too, mister. We'll carry the stretcher by hand," she told her partner.

In no time, the garbage bags were lying in the back of the ambulance. Althea declined a ride. "We'll walk. I'd rather," she said.

"But Althea—" Phineas started to say. He'd never ridden in an ambulance. He thought, if he asked, they might let him ride in back with the mummy, or with the garbage if that was what it turned out to be.

"So would Phineas," Althea said.

His father was talking with the detective, and barely registered what she was saying. He got into Detective Arsenault's car. The ambulance pulled away. The detective pulled away.

"Thanks a lot Althea." Phineas had half a mind to

129

jog all the way to the hospital, to pay her back. "And we'll probably miss the excitement."

"We'll just miss signing forms, and waiting. You've been X-rayed enough, Fin, you know how long it takes. Remember that sprained ankle? We sat around for three hours."

"But when I broke my collarbone falling off the roof it only took—no time at all."

"I want to talk with you," Althea said, ignoring him, setting off. If she wanted to talk with him, why was she ignoring what he said? He fell into step with her anyway.

"I wonder if Dad will have them check to make sure the crown is safe," Althea said.

"Why should he do that?"

"Because Ken says the crown is valuable, and taking the mummy could be only a blind, to distract us, and leave time to get the crown away, and hidden, until it can be sold."

"But it's in the museum safe."

"What if the Batchelors are the ones, though. What if—for example, he could have a duplicate made of the wreath, and then sell it, or use it in some way to get himself a better job. He could go to Egypt and claim to find it there, which would build his reputation. Would you know a fake, if it came back a fake? And she has keys, I bet she even has a copy of the new key to the door, so she could get the mummy out. She'd help him."

"Then why go through the door with a blowtorch?" Phineas thought it was a brilliant point.

"To mislead us. Like we talked about the first time. If the most important thing for her is keeping control over the library; if the library is like her child."

"Wouldn't she worry about getting caught?"

130

"Nobody's ever in the cellars after dark. Even we aren't, and we're the only ones who've been there. They're closed up for the summer. So she could take all the time she needed. Or they could. Nobody would see them, if they took the mummy out the door into the parking lot."

"I can't imagine it, Althea. Your imagination is getting you carried away."

"Then who?"

"Why does it have to be someone we know?"

"It doesn't have to, but it probably is. I don't think it's Dad, do you?"

"*What?*" They were on the sidewalk now, stopped for a light. Phineas just turned to stare at his sister.

"When marriages are in trouble, people begin to act strange. Out of character. Remember Karen's mother, the way she bought an Irish wolfhound? And nobody wanted a dog? Not even her? So who knows what Dad might do."

"I don't think so," Phineas said. He didn't ask Althea if she thought their parents' marriage was in trouble; he didn't want to hear her answer.

"Would he have woken us up leaving the house the last two nights? I'd have heard the car start, I think. I'm not sure. Did you hear him sneaking around at all, Fin? Did you see him asleep in bed?"

"Dad isn't doing crazy things," Phineas said. "I can't prove it, but—we'd know, wouldn't we?"

"Besides, it wouldn't do him any good. The collection is a piece of luck for him. Unless he's feeling self-destructive. What do you think, Fin?"

"I think you're the one who's going crazy."

"It couldn't be you, I know that, because where would you have put it, and you're the one who answered the phone."

131

"Maybe there was no whisperer," Phineas suggested.

"Possible," Althea said. "But I doubt it, I saw your face. Besides, you'd need someone working with you, to make the call so we could go find the mummy, and you don't have any friends here."

"What about Casey?"

"He's not a friend, is he?"

"He might be. I can't tell yet."

"So it's not you or me—because if there was a whisperer you have to know it can't be me. I was right there in the kitchen. I keep wanting to think it's Ken, but that's because I don't like him. I can't think of any reason for him to take the mummy. It's the crown he's interested in."

"For a paper," Phineas said.

"One of his brilliant papers," Althea said.

"So brilliant he'll be offered a job at Harvard." They both snickered.

"Unless he's in collusion with the Batchelors? But that's too many crazy people, don't you think?"

"How about Mr. Vandemark? If he really wants the collection to go to the Boston museum, he might hire some crooks to make trouble. Casey told me—He said they're pretty ruthless, when it comes to the family."

Althea stopped dead. A man ran into her, and apologized, but she barely looked at him. "I never thought of that. That makes sense—how the thief knew about the mummy, and why she had to be returned safely. Because they wouldn't want any damage done. No museum will be interested in damaged pieces, not when they've got undamaged ones. He'd be able to pay someone, whatever the price was, and he looks like the kind of man who thinks that when he wants something that automatically makes it all right."

Now that he thought of Casey's father that way, Phineas could see that it was possible. He felt pretty smart. "Don't forget O'Meara, if she's hungry enough for some story. She could turn this into a mummy's curse thing, she doesn't care very much if it's true, as long as she gets the story."

"I don't think O'Meara would," Althea said.

"How come you're willing to think Mr. Vandemark would but you won't even consider O'Meara?" Phineas answered his own question. "Because she's female."

"Historically, women are victims rather than criminals," Althea said. "I mean, even the mummy. She's female, isn't she? And look what's happened to her."

Phineas was sorry he'd mentioned it. Once she'd started, Althea was almost impossible to stop.

"It's as if you're stuck with the sex you are forever. Even after you're dead. Women are stuck being weak, being victims. All on account of sex."

"Yeah, well, women are as eager for it as men are," Phineas said. He knew he was deliberately misunderstanding her and he meant to. He meant to sound crude too, but once he'd said it he didn't know why he'd said it. He didn't know beans about sex, and he didn't much care. He figured he would care when he got older, but for now all he knew was how to sound crude. And he knew he was faking his crudeness even if nobody else knew. Not even Althea, who was giving him the dirty look he deserved. What if everybody else who sounded like they knew what they were talking about was faking it, just like he was? "I'm sorry, Althea," he said.

"You should be."

"There are always women like Sappho," he said, hoping to change her mood.

"How many like that are there? Out of how many millions?"

They were coming up to the entrance of the emergency room. Out of the ambulances parked in the ambulance bay, Phineas couldn't pick out theirs. He wished he'd never started this conversation with Althea; and he wished she'd just lay off men. "Men go to war," he said.

"Women have babies," she said.

They were walking side by side, but not looking at each other. He suspected, from the sound of her voice, that Althea was finding him just as irritating on the subject as he found her. "So what?" he said, and held open the door for her, sarcastically.

❈ 14 ❈

THEIR FATHER WAS WATCHING FOR THEM. HE LED
them through a door and into one of several curtained
cubicles. No one paid any attention; the doctors and
nurses were busy at their own jobs. In the cubicle, curtains pulled closed, Phineas and Althea stood side by
side at the foot of the bed where the garbage bags lay.
Detective Arsenault stood by the head. Mr. Hall had a
pair of scissors, and started cutting the top bag.

It was bright in the little space, and crowded. The
scissors cut away first one bag and then another. Phineas had forgotten the quarrel, and he thought Althea
had too because she had a hand on his arm, as if having
him beside her made her feel less nervous. Her hand
on his arm made him feel more nervous, as if nervous-
ness was a cold, and he could catch it.

Mr. Hall folded the plastic back off of the shape.
What was revealed by that was a dirty white blanket.
He folded that carefully off, letting it hang down, and
did the same with the dirty blue blanket he found next.
The thief had wrapped her up in blankets. Unwrapped,
the mummy lay on the high hospital bed, like a sacrifice
on an altar, with the black plastic hanging down, and
the white blanket, and the blue.

The mummy had no feet. That was Phineas's first
thought, as his father and Althea drew in whistling
breaths. But that wasn't entirely true. The feet were
flattened, as if somebody had driven over them. Or

smashed, as if someone had clubbed them with a base-ball bat, hammering down on them.

"What's this about?" Detective Arsenault asked. He was bending over to look at the mummy's shoulder.

Mr. Hall crowded around to look. Phineas shifted himself to see, without getting in anyone's way.

A long dark slash gaped behind the portrait panel. Its edges were pushed in slightly, as if someone had tried to shove his hand into the mummy's neck.

"The portrait looks just the same," Phineas said. He said it to cheer himself up, because the sight of the smashed feet and slashed neck sank his spirits. Seri-ously sank his spirits. Even smashed, the mummy didn't smell bad, though; just old, dusty and old. "At least he didn't hurt the portrait."

Somehow, damaging the portrait would have been the worst thing. If the portrait had been defaced, or de-stroyed, or damaged, then she would have been really lost. Really dead, he thought, and he could have laughed at himself. If there was anything deader than a mummy, he'd like to know what. Dead was all you could be, once you died. But still, he felt as if—as long as her face looked up out of the portrait she was only dead. Not really gone, disappeared. He guessed maybe the ancient Egyptians who spent so much time and money on mummies must have felt the same way.

"Was it for the necklace?" Mr. Hall asked.

What necklace? Phineas thought.

"She's wearing one in the portrait, probably uncut emeralds set in gold, according to Ken Simard," Mr. Hall said.

Voices spoke beyond the curtains. Althea stood at the mummy's feet, staring down. Phineas had no idea what she was thinking. Her face was more of a mask than the mummy's portrait. Her two frizzy ponytails stuck

136

out behind her ears like antennae, and it was almost as if Althea were listening to something they were radio-ing in to her.

"Would the mummy have been buried wearing the necklace?" the detective asked.

"Ken said probably not, but it's not impossible. It's just not what they usually did in the Roman era. That's one of the things the X ray would have told us. But Roman era burials weren't like the earlier dynasties, when the tombs were treasure houses, and the mummies were covered with amulets and breastplates, necklaces, scarabs—not to mention the artifacts all around the tombs."

"Like Tutankhamen's tomb," Detective Arsenault said. "So probably the thief was looking for the necklace. That's the way I read this. And when there was no necklace"—his big hand gestured toward the mummy's wounded neck—"he got angry."

"And took it out on the feet?" Mr. Hall asked. "For the same reason that muggers will beat up on someone who doesn't have any money?"

"Or a house will be trashed," the detective agreed.

"But why the feet?" Althea asked. Her voice was a croak, and they all stared at her. She shook her head. She didn't want to be asked any questions, she wouldn't answer.

Phineas looked at the little mound of smashed bones and dehydrated flesh and wrappings that had been the mummy's feet. It was like any other pile of dirt, no more than what you might sweep up from under a re-frigerator that hadn't moved for about a hundred years.

But did they have refrigerators a hundred years ago?

His mind was jumping around. It was as if he didn't want to think about what had happened.

"What do you think, Sam?" the detective asked.

"Could somebody have figured out with this incision that there was no necklace? I assume he didn't find one, the way I read what happened."

Mr. Hall bent down to look more closely at the wound. Without touching the mummy, he held his hand beside the wound, as if imagining. "Maybe. With a small hand? Or long fingers? It would explain why the edges are sort of crushed."

"I wouldn't want to stick my hand in there," the detective said.

Phineas could see what might have happened, and the frustration the thief would have felt after taking all that risk—two nights in a row. He guessed the guy must have been angry, with all the disappointment. Angry enough to want to destroy something.

"What puzzles me," the detective said, "is just what you asked, Althea. Why the feet?"

Althea nodded, her lips pushed tightly together as if they would quiver if she left them alone. She was seriously upset, Phineas thought. He didn't blame her.

"Why not smash the whole thing, if that's the way it happened," the detective said, musing. "Why call you, to tell you where it was? Why wrap it up so carefully?"

Mr. Hall shrugged. "I suppose we should be grateful," he said. "And I am." But he didn't sound it.

Althea turned on her heels, and pushed her way through the curtains. Nobody tried to stop her.

"I am grateful it hasn't been entirely destroyed," Mr. Hall said. "But it was perfect, and now it's—" The more he said, the more he sounded angry. "The damage is irreversible, irremediable."

Phineas knew what his father meant. If he'd ever had a dog, and anyone had ever run over it, he'd feel this way. He blinked his eyes.

The mummy's sad face smiled up at the ceiling light, as if she knew what had happened.

"At least, it hasn't been destroyed," the detective suggested.

"But she was perfect before," Mr. Hall snapped back. "I get so sick of this century, or this country—'Look on the bright side.' If someone dies, the first thing anyone asks is 'Are you getting over it?' If a marriage breaks up, the first question is 'Are you dating anyone?' It does, it makes me sick. It disgusts me. Sorry, I'm just—"

"No, I understand," the detective said. He was looking at Phineas's father with an alert expression that made Phineas wonder if his father was a chief suspect. "I do, or I think I do. Listen, Sam, I'd like—if you'd like—would you come for dinner some night? With the kids, a family dinner."

"I'd like that." Phineas's father was pleased.

"I'll talk to my wife and call you."

He must not suspect Mr. Hall, Phineas thought. You wouldn't invite someone you suspected of a crime to your house for dinner.

"I'll be seeing you soon anyway, to sign statements. Although, I have to tell you, I don't think we'll ever find the man who did this. Or woman, it could be a woman."

Unless that was exactly what you'd do, so your suspect would relax his guard.

The mummy lay under the bright light, looking out under her portrait. She didn't know that after more than fifteen hundred years of being perfect she was now ruined. No matter what anyone did, she could never be perfect again.

Phineas minded that. He knew there was nothing to do about it, but he couldn't stop minding.

❖ 15 ❖

By the time the mummy had been X-rayed and returned to the collection room in the cellar of the library, it was midafternoon. As soon as they got home, Phineas went to work making sandwiches for his father and himself. His father ate without saying anything, and then sat staring at the wooden tabletop while Phineas cleaned up. "Why don't you go up and take a nap, Dad?" Phineas finally suggested.

His father smiled, but not as if he was about to laugh. "I'm waiting for Mr. Vandemark's phone call. So, Phineas, how do you think we'll like living on the West Coast?"

"Are we going to move?"

"After they fire me."

"Why should they do that? It's not your fault there was a thief around who wanted to steal the necklace."

"People like having someone to blame," his father explained.

"There's no way you could have prevented it. Is there?"

"Sure there is. I could have hired round-the-clock security, or I could have camped out in the room. Especially after the first attempt."

"Yeah, but the guy would probably have brained you. The way he did the mummy's feet."

"Can you brain feet?" his father asked. It was pretty

140

feeble, for a joke, but at least it was a try. "Oh, well, I can go back to tending bar."

"You're a teacher, not a bartender."

"Don't underestimate me, Phineas. I put myself through school tending bar, and I'm pretty good at it. The difficulty is, when you've been fired, it's hard to get another job. People wonder why you were fired."

"That doesn't make sense," Phineas said.

"The world doesn't make sense," his father said dismally.

"No, I was thinking about the necklace. Who knew about it? I know, anyone who read O'Meara's article—"

"Bless her pointed little heart," Mr. Hall murmured.

"—but, Dad, he could have looked for it right there, he didn't have to take the mummy out. Why would he kidnap the mummy? And don't tell me you can't kidnap a mummy, okay?" Phineas said, just to get his father to smile again.

A knock on the screen door interrupted them. Mr. Hall didn't look interested, so Phineas went to answer it. A tall, broad-shouldered man stood there, athletic looking despite his khaki suit, with long legs and narrow hips; he was some kind of businessman, with the tie. For a few seconds, Phineas didn't recognize him.

"Ken?" he said, opening the door. Behind Ken's shoulder, he could see a taxi waiting.

"I just came to say good-bye, and good luck," Ken said. He stepped into the hallway. "I hope your father is home."

"In the kitchen."

Phineas followed Ken down the hall. Something was different. "You shaved your beard," he realized. He moved around to look at Ken from the front. The skin the beard had covered was paler than the rest of Ken's

141

face. He'd left the mustache, but trimmed, as his hair had been trimmed. "You look—" Phineas couldn't figure out how to say it.

"Better," Ken suggested with a laugh.

"Let me see," Mr. Hall asked.

Ken turned around and flexed his muscles, fists raised in the traditional strongman pose. Then he turned his profile, and swung his arms down, one flexed in back, one flexed in front, and posed briefly that way. Then he relaxed and smiled. "I have a lucky feeling about this trip. Although I hate to abandon you when things are such a mess, Sam. I heard about the mummy."

"It'll sort itself out. At the moment, I'm not feeling too sanguine."

Ken's face sobered. "I can imagine. But I'll be back in a month, and at your disposal."

"If I'm still here."

His father looked small, sitting there, shoulders slumped, small especially compared to Ken. His father looked small and weak. Phineas didn't like seeing his father look that way.

"They can't fire you, Sam. You've got a contract."

His father smiled. "Life is full of surprises."

"You'd better be here when I get back," Ken said. "Whatever happens, don't do anything until I get back. I won't let them fire you. You're too good a teacher." He looked, as he said it, as if nothing would stand in his way, because he could take care of anything. Phineas was surprised at the difference shaving his beard made in Ken.

"Thanks for the vote of confidence," Mr. Hall said.

"You know as well as I do there's nothing you could have done," Ken announced. "But I really have to go. I've got a plane to catch. See you, Phineas." He shook

142

Phineas's hand. "Sam." He shook Mr. Hall's hand. "Is Althea around? I'd like to say good-bye to her."

Phineas went up to get Althea, but she wasn't in her room. Opening the door, he saw the bed—made, of course—and the empty desk, a single light like a spotlight on the papers spread over it. He ran back downstairs. "She's not here."

"Where is she?" Mr. Hall asked.

"I don't know," Phineas answered.

"Probably off with some boyfriend," Ken said. "I wouldn't worry if I were you. When she turns up, tell her I wanted to say good-bye, will you?"

They walked out onto the porch to watch Ken set off. He turned to wave before he climbed into the taxi. The taxi pulled away.

"What a difference," Phineas said. "He looks like a businessman, a successful businessman. Doesn't he?"

"Or a successful politician," Mr. Hall answered. "Althea wasn't in her room?"

Phineas shook his head. "It looked like she had been there, working, because of the papers on her desk. Maybe she heard Ken and didn't want to see him?"

"She's hiding out in the bathroom? I doubt it. Probably, she went to get us something for dinner. Women like to soothe men with food."

"They do?"

"Your mother does. And it works. Don't underestimate feminine wisdom, Phineas; a lobster would make me feel a whole lot better about the world at this point. Let's hope Althea's gone out to get lobster."

Phineas opened the drawer where they kept grocery money and counted it. "There's forty dollars. Has she taken money?"

His father was sitting at the table again. He looked up at Phineas, but Phineas didn't feel like he was being looked at. The laugh lines on his father's face looked like worry lines. "I can't remember."

Phineas sat down to face it. "You're worried too," he said.

"Of course I am. I'm not even sure there won't be a third attempt."

"Because it's not like her to just—disappear."

"I don't know how much blame President Blight will put on me. I don't even know if he's the kind of man who always blames someone. I don't know anything about him, or anyone up here."

"And it's been over two hours since we've seen her."

"Althea?" his father asked. "She's fifteen, Fin, she's smart, it's Maine, not New York. Kids her age love being alone, feeling alone, taking solitary walks."

Phineas relaxed. His father was right.

By six, neither of them was relaxed, and by eight both of them were moving fitfully around the house, going out to the porch to look up and down the road, sitting on the stairs to be close to the phone. Phineas finally went back up to Althea's room, thinking maybe she'd left them a note up there, maybe he should have looked more carefully the first time he went up. He went straight to the desk.

Pieces of lined papers were sort of scattered around, filled with Greek letters, and some of the awkward sentences that identified them as attempts at translation. "If the leader would have the tents of the (cruel? bad? vengeful?) enemy known . . ." The gooseneck lamp shone like a spotlight on the paper she must have been working on last. But all that was written on it were some mazelike doodles, and words in English. Phineas read his own name, and his heart rose. Phineas, he read, So If Mom Asks Request Divorce.

His heart sank. Underneath, she had written more

144

sloppily Kill Every Noodle, and crossed it out with a single stroke.

It didn't make any sense. Althea didn't want their parents to get divorced, did she? He'd have said she didn't, but he guessed she might. If they did get divorced, then Althea and Phineas wouldn't have to worry whether they were going to. If they did, then Althea wouldn't have to cope with the question of if there was anything she should do to stop them.

But killing noodles was seriously weird. If that was what came out of her hand when she was doodling, he was going to think that there was something wrong with Althea. You couldn't even kill noodles. They weren't even alive. You couldn't kill anything unless it was alive. He wished Althea would come home, so he could ask her.

Downstairs, his father was talking on the phone, which hadn't rung. Phineas came out of Althea's room, turning off the light, but his father had hung up before Phineas could hear what he'd been saying. Mr. Hall turned around. "I called the police. They're sending someone over."

The two of them waited in restless silence until a knock at the door announced the arrival of a policewoman with shining blond hair. They hadn't turned on any lights, so Phineas did that while she introduced herself as Officer Gable and said yes, if it was already made she'd like a cup of coffee, with milk and sugar if they had it. She sat down at the table and took out her notebook. Phineas sat next to his father at the round table.

"It's your daughter who's missing?" Officer Gable asked.

They both nodded.

"I am sorry," she said, and sounded like she meant

145

that. "Often, there's some simple explanation. How long has she been gone?"

"We haven't seen her since about two this afternoon," Mr. Hall said.

"How old is she?"

"Fifteen."

"Ah, fifteen," the officer murmured, as if now things were beginning to make sense. "Did you have a quarrel?"

They both shook their heads.

"Her mother?"

"My wife is living in Oregon. As far as I know, she hasn't called today, or recently. I suppose she could have, before we got back?" He turned to Phineas.

"Althea would have left a note," Phineas said.

"You've called the homes of her friends?" the officer asked.

"We just moved up here. She doesn't have any friends. The only place she might have been is the college library, but that closed three hours ago. Over three hours ago."

The officer had pale blue eyes, and she looked sternly through them at Mr. Hall to ask her next question. "Has she run away before?"

They both shook their heads.

"Did she leave any note?"

Phineas found his voice again. "I went up to her room, and all there was was some doodling, and her work. She's studying Greek," he explained to the officer. "Ancient Greek. She studies a lot." The officer nodded sympathetically at him, to encourage him to keep talking. "We leave notes for one another down here, on this table, where they'll be noticed."

It was funny, the officer's sympathy made him feel better, because she was taking them seriously. But by

146

taking them seriously she was making him even more nervous. He kept wanting to swallow.

"I think the first thing is to radio a description to all the squad cars, in case anyone sees her. It's Althea Hall, correct? Age fifteen. Height?"

"Five three or four," Mr. Hall said. "Weight, I don't know, but she's chunky, solid."

"What was she wearing, when you last saw her?"

The *blatt-blatt* of the phone interrupted the questions and answers. Mr. Hall jumped up to answer it, but returned to send Officer Gable to the phone. She spoke briefly before coming back into the kitchen. She didn't sit down. Her cheeks were pink and she seemed angry. "You didn't tell me you were already involved in another investigation. You didn't tell me you were working with Detective Arsenault."

"I'm sorry," Mr. Hall said meekly.

"What difference does that make?" Phineas demanded.

She didn't answer. "Detective Arsenault wants you to come downtown. I'll stay here, in case there's a phone call, or Althea comes home. Until you return, I'll be here. You should have told me you were involved in the mummy theft."

"This doesn't have anything to do with the mummy," Phineas said, but as soon as the words were out of his mouth he wondered if that was true. It didn't make sense. But nothing about the mummy had made sense, all along, or about the collection—if that was what was causing everything. Phineas didn't want to think about it. He didn't know how to think about it. He just wanted somebody to make it all all right. And he thought his mother ought to be there with them to help out. He knew he couldn't blame her—she didn't even know what was going on, she was thousands of miles away, but—

He hurried after his father, who was already heading out the door to the car.

Phineas had never been inside a police station before, although he'd seen plenty of them on TV. It had a lot in common with a hospital, he thought—both of them big spaces filled with people doing their jobs. Detective Arsenault's office had glass walls facing the desk-filled central area; Phineas guessed that the windows were there because if somebody pulled a gun everybody would see what was happening. Detective Arsenault stood up and waved his hand at two wooden chairs. Phineas sat down and waited for the detective to explain everything, and tell them were Althea was. Otherwise, why would he call them down to the station?

"Why didn't you call me?" Detective Arsenault asked Mr. Hall. "When did you know she was missing?"

Phineas slumped down in his chair. The detective didn't know any more than they did.

"I'm sorry, Sam," the detective said. He straightened his glasses and slumped into his own chair behind the desk. "I have kids of my own. Missing kids—that gets me where it hurts."

"Yes, exactly," Mr. Hall said.

"Sam, is it possible she's run away to be with her mother? I know it's an awkward question, but—might she have?"

"I suppose." Phineas's father rubbed at his eyes. "The way I feel right now, anything could have happened. I don't care what as long as Althea's all right. But how would she plan to get across the country?"

"Hitchhike? Or, does she have any money? Buses don't cost all that much, have you tried the bus station?"

148

Phineas exploded. "Althea wouldn't. That would be—crazy—and she doesn't do crazy things. You don't understand. This was something we talked over. A decision we all made. It was a choice. Althea doesn't back down on something she's thought about and decided. Besides, she's angry at Mom, she blames her. So she wouldn't go to see her."

"Even if something happened she desperately wanted to run away from?"

Phineas shook his head. Nothing had happened, except the mummy and everything related to the mummy.

"Then where else might she go?"

"Nowhere!" Phineas practically yelled. He didn't know why the detective was being so dumb. "That's why we're worried!"

Detective Arsenault looked at him from behind glasses, sympathetic and patient. "Kids Althea's age, teenagers—you never know what they'll get up to. Girls especially."

"She's too smart," Phineas said.

"Nobody's too smart, Phineas," the detective warned him. "Especially not someone who's sure he is. If you take my meaning."

Phineas took it, and he agreed. Not just about kids, either. Grown-ups acted as if kids were stupider than adults, acted superior, but as far as he was concerned it was a tie match.

"If, however, she hasn't run away, we have to consider the other possibilities," the detective said.

"Other than something connected with the mummy," Mr. Hall said. "And I can't see what connection with the mummy there could be."

Detective Arsenault nodded. "Kidnap, rape, suicide—I'm sorry, Sam, but those are the choices."

"I know. Don't think I haven't thought of that."

149

Phineas hadn't. His stomach felt like it was trying to climb up into his chest.

"Or running away," the detective said. "Neither of you can think of any reason?"

They shook their heads.

"Phineas, you wouldn't keep secrets for her, would you? In a situation like this?"

"She doesn't have any secrets. Or if she does, I don't know them. If you're thinking of drugs," Phineas said, finally figuring out what the detective might be hinting at, "you're wrong."

"Sometimes a family doesn't suspect," the detective said.

"But we would," Phineas told him.

The detective looked at him, waiting, brown eyes behind big glasses.

"I'd tell you," Phineas said. "I would."

Detective Arsenault decided to believe him. "All right. But it would have been simpler. I think we ought to plan for all possibilities. We'll radio a description to the patrol cars. Phineas, you'll wait at home, in case she calls. If she does, or if there's a phone call—"

"From a kidnapper? Who'd want to kidnap Althea? She's not rich."

"You call the station, right away. Do you understand that?"

Phineas nodded.

"And, Sam, I thought you and I would get in your car, which isn't a police car, to check out the places where kids tend to gather. Just in case."

Mr. Hall nodded.

"Because"—the detective looked from Phineas to his father—"if Althea was the one who took the mummy, and damaged it—People do some very strange things," he said, to both of them. "A policeman learns

150

that. Once you know the motives, things make sense, but before that things often look senseless. If Althea is the thief, she'll be feeling guilty, and afraid—"

"You mean, she could be a lot more upset than she's shown, about her mother and me," Mr. Hall asked. "Phineas, do you think she is?"

"Of course she is, but that doesn't mean she'd go crazy. We're all more upset than we're showing." Phineas was out of patience with both of them. His father at least should know better. But his father was too frightened to be thinking clearly. Phineas wondered if he also was too frightened to think clearly. "She was doodling about divorce," he remembered. "But, Dad, I can't believe Althea would do all that. Be crazy enough to do all that. And us not notice. Can you believe that?"

"It makes some kind of sense, at least," Mr. Hall answered. "I almost want to believe it, because it does make sense."

"Let's get going," Detective Arsenault said, getting up from his desk. "I'll send you home in a squad car, Phineas. Officer Gable will be there when you arrive, but she can't stay. Will you be all right alone?"

"I'll be fine," Phineas said. He had trouble thinking of Althea as crazy enough to break into the library, twice, to steal the mummy—and with a blowtorch which she had no idea how to use?—and what about that whispered phone call, when Althea was in the kitchen? He had trouble thinking of Althea as someone whose way of dealing with trouble was to run away. "I'm fine."

And he didn't believe she would, not for a minute.

✦ 16 ✦

Phineas rode alone in the back of the police car, through bright city streets, then onto less lighted residential streets, then into the darkness of the college campus. Among the dark shapes of empty houses, his own porch light shone brightly, and dim yellow light showed through the glass panes of the door. A police car was parked in front of their house; the police car he was riding in drove away; with all these police cars, they *had* to find Althea.

Phineas didn't care where she was, or how she'd gotten there, as long as she got back home. Once she was home, they could deal with any other problems. Getting her home, safe—

Officer Gable hurried out of the kitchen as he let himself in the door. "It's you," she said.

"I'm sorry," Phineas said.

"Nothing here, no phone calls," she reported. Phineas nodded. "I have to go back downtown," Officer Gable said. Phineas nodded. "Is there anyone I could call, to come stay with you?" she asked.

"I'm fine, I'll be fine," Phineas said. He didn't need her standing there feeling sorry for him, when Althea needed to be found.

"Do you have someone you can call, if you—feel like you need someone?" she asked. She was turning her hat around and around in her hands.

"Yeah," Phineas said. It wasn't a lie. He could al-

152

ways call his mother—for all the good that would do. He shut the door behind her.

Phineas got about one-third of the way up the stairs before he turned around. Sat down. Put his knees together and rested his elbows on his knees, chin on his hands.

He had no reason for sitting down. But then, he had no reason for going up into the darkness or down into the light.

Sitting on the stairs, waiting, was pretty familiar. It was how he waited when he had a friend coming over, or it was Christmas morning and not time yet to fetch the stockings. He sat on the stairs—except those stairs had carpeting running up them, they were a lot softer— listening to his parents last spring, arguing out solutions for the dilemma. Sitting on the stairs, waiting, was always solitary. Last spring, Althea had already started to close herself in her room and bury her nose in a Greek book.

He wished he *could* call his mother. He could call her, he knew the number. But it wouldn't do any good. What could she do, all the way across the country and probably—he subtracted three hours from the time— having dinner, probably having dinner out with someone, arguing out some proposal, or networking. He had no idea where his mother was. He could no more find her than he knew where Althea—

Blatt-blatt.

Phineas jumped, and was on the ground floor without his feet touching any of the steps. He picked up the phone. "Phineas?" a woman's voice asked, and he almost said *Mom.* Before he could say anything, the voice asked, "Is your father there? It's O'Meara."

"No. He's out."

153

"You're alone?"

"Yes." So what's it to you? was in his voice.

"Althea hasn't turned up?"

"No." He wondered how she knew.

"You don't have any idea—"

"No. Listen, I've gotta go, we can't tie up the phone." He didn't want to talk to anyone, but he especially didn't want to talk to O'Meara. Who had started all of this with her dumb newspaper story. Who didn't care about anything except getting a story. "Okay? Good-bye," and he dropped the receiver onto its cradle without giving her any chance to say anything. She didn't know how people felt.

How Phineas felt, right then, was seriously bad.

He didn't want to think about it. Thinking about it didn't do any good. He could have gone up, gone to sleep maybe, or gone to eat, or gone to watch TV, but he didn't. It was as if there was a wide foggy space between anything he might think of doing and his body that would do it. He sat on the stairs, on the bottom step this time, waiting. Not thinking about anything.

Footsteps on the front step. He raised his head and saw right away it wasn't Althea. It was too thin for Althea, and it wasn't running the way Althea would be if she were coming home, to explain and apologize for whatever—

The second knock on the door he answered. O'Meara stood there, so he let her in. Before she was through the door she was talking away. "I know I'm intruding. You don't have to pretend I'm not. I just didn't like to think of you alone here. When I heard about Althea—"

"What about her?" Phineas was suddenly entirely alert.

"On the police radio. They broadcast her description and name."

"Oh." Energy went out of him just as suddenly and completely as it had exploded in him.

O'Meara looked closely at him. "I'm sorry, Phineas. But the good news is, this isn't New York. Or Los Angeles. Or Boston, Detroit, New Orleans . . . Besides, it doesn't do any good to worry—"

By then she was in the kitchen, putting her big bag down on the table, turning around to ask him, "Where is your father? I'm going to make a mug of tea, is that all right? Do you want something, Phineas? Tea? Milk? Hot chocolate?"

He shook his head. He sat down at the table. She moved around the kitchen and he didn't even bother looking to see what she was up to. He felt like he had a body, but he wasn't connected to it. He felt the way the mummy might feel, with a body that didn't count for anything, and her face a portrait on wood, still looking out but having nothing to do with her body at all. And somebody smashing away at her feet.

Weird, he felt weird.

O'Meara put a mug of hot chocolate down in front of him. She sat down facing him, dipping her tea bag up and down in her mug.

"Everybody runs away at least once," O'Meara said.

Phineas shook his head. Not true. He never had, and out of all the people he knew, only two had ever, and there were maybe three older siblings who had. That wasn't everybody.

O'Meara's face looked like a cat when it's trying to be friendly, but doesn't know how because it's a cat. "Okay, I know it's not everyone, it's not even a majority, it's just lots of people who do. I was just trying to make you feel better."

"Althea wouldn't run away," Phineas said. His voice sounded normal to him, which was a relief.

"But if she didn't, then what has happened to her?" O'Meara asked. She was sorry right away she'd said that. "Isn't there any clue?"

"There was something on her desk that looked like a note. To me, my name is on it, but it's just doodling. That's all. She just left the hospital, when we were there with the mummy after we'd found her. When the mummy was being X-rayed. Althea just walked out."

O'Meara stirred her tea and sipped from the spoon. "Can I see it?"

See what? Phineas wondered. Now what was she talking about? Although, he ought to admit it, it did feel better not to be sitting alone on the stairs, waiting.

"Phineas? Are you in there? Can I see the note to you? Can you get it? Or can I?"

Phineas got up from the table and went up the stairs to Althea's room. He picked up the sheet of paper and decided to leave the light on. Althea was afraid of the dark.

Dumb, it was dumb and he knew it. That was a dumb reason for doing anything, especially something useless, but he let himself go ahead and do it because at least it was something.

O'Meara studied the paper. She read it a couple of times. She turned it upside down and sideways. She held it up to the light and looked through it. "I guess you're right," she finally said. "That's just nonsense, Kill Every Noodle. You might as well say Kiss Eddie Noonan."

"Or Klingons Envy No One," Phineas said. He blinked his eyes, furious.

"I'm so sorry, Phineas," O'Meara said. He could feel coming out of her, as real as if you could actually see it, a warm protective feeling. A mother feeling. His friends' mothers had said that to him, "I'm so sorry," in just that soft voice, had poured that feeling over him, when they heard he was moving. He hated it. It made him choke up, and he didn't want to sit around, choked up. His friends were much easier to deal with, they just said "That sucks," and kicked something.

"This sucks," Phineas said. He didn't have room to kick the table, so he gulped down some hot chocolate.

"It's okay with me if you feel like crying," O'Meara said. "I don't blame you, I feel like crying too."

She wasn't all bad, Phineas guessed. A few tears had trickled out, and he brushed them away.

"I'll never tell anyone you're not perfectly macho," O'Meara said with a little smile, her own eyes filming over with tears. "Just think of me as an aunt. Someone you know, someone safe, your favorite aunt."

"Okay," Phineas said, smiling himself at the thought of his mother's sister, Aunt Liz, a small, neat woman with huge eyes and curly hair, a lawyer. "The lawyer who ate Milwaukee," they called her. She was seriously awe inspiring and about the opposite of what O'Meara was thinking of.

"Divorce is always hard on the children," O'Meara said now, her finger on the message Phineas was supposed to give his mother. This time she didn't look at him. "She sounds upset about it."

"There isn't any divorce," Phineas said.

"Then why isn't your mother here?"

"She got a job offer," he said. "In Oregon."

"But you didn't go with her," O'Meara pointed out, as if he didn't know that.

"Dad got this job offer."

O'Meara nodded her head. "I can dig it. How come you kids are with your dad?"

157

"We all talked it over." O'Meara was nosy, but she was all right, Phineas decided. Besides, it was easier to have the air filled with words than with the silence of unnamed fears. "Since Dad was on a school schedule it's easier for him to take care of us—and Mom's working for a congressman, which means irregular hours, and being home less of the time."

"Which congressman?"

"Harlow."

"You're kidding."

Phineas shook his head.

"You're serious."

Phineas nodded his head.

"Oh, wow. Is she ever going to come here, so I can meet her and find out what he's really like?"

Phineas didn't know. And didn't care. "What I'm trying to say is, Althea isn't upset, or, at least, she understands the reasons. She was part of the decision. She could have gone with Mom."

"Maybe it's easier when you're married," O'Meara said. "My boyfriend—I just broke up with him, two months ago, after being together more than a year, so we were serious—he wanted me to quit my job and go to Florida with him. And get married, it's not as if he was trying to take advantage. But I have this job. . . ." She took a swallow of tea. "Anyhow, if you all agreed on this, how come Althea's telling you to ask your mom to get a divorce?"

Phineas didn't know. "She doesn't mean it." Unless, of course, she did. "She blames people, she likes to know whose fault something is, she likes to be sure of that."

"So she blames your mother?"

"Yeah."

"What about you?"

158

"I don't blame anyone."

"Come off it, Phineas," O'Meara said in that superior, grown-up, I-know-better-than-you voice.

Phineas wasn't going to let her get away with that. "I'm twelve years old, I'm just a kid," he said. "I'm a twelve-year-old kid—as long as the icebox is full I'll be happy." He sounded like a wiseass, he knew; but that was better than sounding like a wimp. "The marriage is their problem, not mine. I've got problems of my own. Like, Althea."

"Who is so unhappy she ran away."

A seriously dumb remark. Phineas knew that Althea wouldn't run away, as surely as he knew it was now 9:50. He just shook his head. "She didn't."

"But if she didn't, then where is she?" O'Meara pointed out again.

"That's what I'm worried about!" Phineas yelled. He pushed his chair back from the table. He stomped out of the kitchen, stomped into the living room, jerked on the TV, and sat down in a chair in front of it. O'Meara stayed in the kitchen, which was lucky, because if she'd followed him he'd have really yelled at her.

The moving pictures, in color, with sound, played in the box, but he didn't really see them and whatever noise they were making didn't penetrate his ears. Between his ears, there was a dead land. Like the no-man's-land of World War I. Yellow light fell down over him, and he sprawled out across the overstuffed chair as if he were watching TV.

The phone woke him. *Blatt-blatt*, it sat him up in his chair. *Blatt-blatt*, but before he'd collected himself to answer it O'Meara already had it.

"No, he's not in," she said. "May I take a message?

I guess you could call me the baby-sitter, if you want to. At the moment that's what I'm doing."

The TV had been turned off. It felt like about midnight. His father hadn't come home. O'Meara hung up the phone and came to the door of the living room. "She didn't leave her name. I've got to go, Phineas. There are a couple of stories I have to write for the morning edition. Do you want me to come back? After?"

"No." He sat up and rubbed his head behind the right ear. "No, thanks. But thanks."

"I've left my number, home and at the paper, right by the phone." She had her bag over her shoulder. "If you hear anything, I sure would like a call."

Phineas nodded.

"Can I come back tomorrow? In the morning?" It was the first time he'd ever heard her sound unsure.

"Yeah, of course," he said. He would have said more, but he was wishing her out of the house. It wasn't that he didn't appreciate her coming by, but he was beginning to have an idea and her questions distracted him. His idea was that if he were going to kidnap Althea, there would be a reason.

O'Meara left.

So if he could think of a reason, Phineas thought—

Blatt-blatt. He shot out of the chair and ran to get the phone. But it was only his father. "I'm at the police station. Are you all right?"

"Fine," Phineas answered. Neither one of them needed to ask if the other had heard anything.

"I'm going to stay here."

"Okay," Phineas said. "I'll hold the fort here."

At least he knew where his father was.

Phineas went back to the living room but didn't turn on the TV. He'd almost had an idea. He closed his eyes

160

to try to chase it down again. Having to do with kidnapping, and with motive. And for some reason he kept remembering what his father had said—days ago, Phineas couldn't place how many days ago—about effect preceding cause.

But what effect? And what cause? He wished he was good at thinking. He felt like he was trying to run down a rabbit, to catch it with his bare hands. If you had a weapon it was easier to bring down a rabbit. Rabbits ran faster than he could. Trying to run a rabbit down, with your bare hands . . .

The next time Phineas woke up, it was deep night. Maybe one-thirty, he thought. He didn't know why he bothered thinking that, because he knew what he was going to do. He knew where he might find Althea. He didn't know how he knew. He didn't care where the idea had come from. He didn't even wonder whether he was right or wrong. He just knew where to look.

He was out of the house and running under dark trees and a dark star-filled sky, with no further thought.

❈ 17 ❈

HALFWAY THERE, PHINEAS STOPPED DEAD IN HIS tracks.

He needed a flashlight. He'd never be able to find her without a flashlight. He ran back home.

In the kitchen, he took his father's big Maglite out of a drawer. He was panting as he ran out of the house again. The screen door slammed shut behind him. He could have jogged for hours and never gotten out of breath, but running full out was taking it out of him.

He slowed down and ran at a jog. The sense of urgency was mostly his own nerves. It was the same feeling he had when he played soccer and he was trying to work the ball down the field for a goal, a hurry *up* feeling that would come over him, no matter how much time there was left in the half. He made himself breathe deeply. Plenty of time, he told himself.

He jogged through darkness along the path, between tall leafy trees and tall bushy evergreens. Buildings loomed up ahead of him, dark black squares. He ran between them and up to the largest blackest square, the library.

Phineas stood at the foot of the steps, looking at the locked doors. He could have hit himself in the head with the flashlight.

He hadn't thought.

He should have called his father, who had a key.

He never thought ahead, thought things out.

And now what could he do?

Just what the thief had done. The big windows to the reading room had stone ledges at their bottoms. He'd break a pane of glass and unhook the window. The thief hadn't had to break it, but he would. He'd tell Mrs. Batchelor, and he just about knew what she'd say, and he was sorry but—

By then, he'd jammed the flashlight into the waist of his jeans and was shoving through the bushes. The ledge was about shoulder height, and stuck out a good six inches, wide enough to stand on, once he'd—with both hands, his sneaker toes clambering at the bricks for purchase—gotten up so his weight rested on his hands on the ledge. He worked a knee up, and onto it, until he was kneeling on it.

With one hand on the bricks that framed the window, as if he could actually hold on, he used the other to pull the long flashlight out of his jeans. Gently, he thought, but even if he fell over backward the bushes would cushion him. Think, he told himself, and because he thought he remembered that the windows lifted up, like the tall windows in old-fashioned school rooms, with catches at the center. He hung the flashlight over his right shoulder, and swung it forward.

Nothing happened. He tipped his head back, looked at the pane of glass he was aiming for, and swung again, an overhead smash.

A cracking sound, and he swung again. It would make a mess on the floor, but he had sneakers on, he'd be okay. He put the flashlight back into his jeans.

He reached in and stretched his hand up. His hand reached in through the broken pane, reached in, and up again, and twisted until his fingers could feel along the top of the window. His fingers found the latch, and figured out how to slip it open.

Phineas pushed up at the top of the broken pane, carefully, using the back of his forearm. Sharpness moved against his skin, but didn't penetrate. The window rose a little.

He pulled his arm back and slid his foot into the narrow opening at the bottom. Gently, he bent his knee to lift his foot to lift the window.

It slid smoothly up. Well made, he thought, and well maintained. Not nearly as hard to move as you'd think from its size it might be. He bent his left knee, letting his left hand run down the bricks, and got first his right leg, then his left, and then, sliding down over the low shelves under the windows, his whole body into the reading room.

It was creepy, the big empty room filled with books and magazines and newspapers, but he didn't need the flashlight to cross it and get out through the big doors. It was the emptiness that made it creepy, the sense of the whole empty building, around and above and below him. It was an ominous silence, a dangerous, hostile silence. A waiting silence. He could hear himself breathing.

His breath came faster, shorter.

Stop, Phineas said to himself. Think. Keys, he told himself, thinking about what it was he wanted to do. He crossed in front of the checkout desk and entered the librarian's office. If the door had been locked, he'd have had to break another window—but the door wasn't locked. Mrs. Batchelor's desk was a flat clear surface, with a tall wooden chair behind it. Phineas pulled out the central drawer and aimed his flashlight into it. Paper clips, marking pens, thumbtacks, piles of library cards—he closed the drawer.

He felt like James Bond, working silently in the solitary darkness, flicking his light on when he needed it, then off for secrecy. He felt like he knew what he was doing. The top right drawer had stationery with the college emblem on top of each sheet. Phineas opened the top left drawer next. He was willing to bet keys would be kept in a top drawer. It was the kind of thing Bond would know. The light flicked on and there they were, three keys on a ring. Phineas grabbed them and turned off the flashlight.

Because he didn't know who might see him, he didn't want to be seen.

He closed the drawer, then left the office, pulling the door closed behind him. Nobody would ever know he'd been there.

Except for fingerprints, he reminded himself. It wasn't as if he ought to be feeling so awfully smart.

Yeah, but it wasn't as if he was a real thief, anyway. He was just seeing what it felt to feel like one.

Phineas unlocked the door to the stairway, and went through. The heavy metal door swung closed behind him, latching itself. The darkness in the stairway was as thick as fog. Phineas was almost surprised to see that the beam of light from the flashlight wasn't murky. Flashlight shining on the steps, keys in his right hand, he went on down.

At the foot of the stairs, one hand on the cool railing, Phineas stopped again. He needed to think. If you knew you made mistakes because you didn't think ahead, then you ought to plan for that. He didn't know exactly how many rooms there were, down here in the cellars. He didn't know what the map of the corridors looked like. He knew how to get from the parking lot entrance to the collection room, room 015, and that was all he knew.

But Althea wouldn't be in the collection room. He was willing to bet on that. In the collection room she'd be found right away, practically. If Althea was down here, and he had a feeling she was, it wasn't so that she could be found right away.

How come he thought that? How come he was so sure of it? It wasn't James Bond he was thinking like, it was the criminal. How come he was thinking like a criminal?

His feet had brought him to the parking lot entrance, which put him at one far corner of the rectangular cellar. Trying to think.

First find Althea, he told himself, then you can pay attention to your criminal talents. He heard his own voice whispering the words.

He knew why he was whispering to himself. It was because it was so creepy, so dark and silent, with only the flashlight beam lighting his way. All he could see was the area of light, on the linoleum floor and flowing up onto cinder block walls painted white. Every nerve cell on the outside of his body was quivering. He felt as if all of his nerves had rushed to the edges of his body and were waiting there, alert for trouble.

Fear, he thought, this must be fear. Serious fear.

He hadn't ever imagined that fear would feel like this, making it hard to think about anything else. Live and learn. He heard his own voice saying that, and he tried to laugh.

The flashlight lit a doorway. He was just standing in front of a door, staring at it. Like all the other doors, this one was flat and painted white. Only a handle, with a key slot at its center, told you it was a door. Phineas stiffened his shoulders and pulled them forward, to loosen the muscles across his back. He blew out a breath of air, in a whooshing sound. He'd been holding his breath too.

"Okay," he said, not even whispering. The darkness

swallowed up his voice. He shouldn't have spoken out loud.

The question was how to find her. What he had thought was that he would go to the cellars and find her. He hadn't really thought. His trouble was that his natural inclination was to go for a service ace, whomp, and take the point. But this game wasn't tennis and couldn't be played that way.

In the mazelike corridors he'd get lost, disoriented. Down here he had no sense of direction. All the corridors looked the same, all the floors looked the same, there was no landmark. But there was, he realized, a series of numbers. All the rooms were numbered. Numbers never duplicated themselves. Numbers were always different. Numbers wouldn't get him lost. All he'd have to do is remember which ones he'd counted.

Phineas didn't know if he could do that. This was like a game of Grandmother's Trunk, but it wasn't a game.

He didn't even know how many rooms there were, except there were more than fifteen—since the collection room was number 015. "So start with oh-oh-one," he whispered to himself. "Jerk."

To his left lay 001, the number painted beside the door, and he got started. He took the three keys, and his first try was the right one. The door opened. Phineas followed his flashlight into a boxlike room.

He used the beam of light the way he'd use his eyes, really looking for something. At floor level, he lit the entire edge of the room, all four sides. Then he did the same thing at shoulder level. This looked like an office, with a desk in the middle and a couple of chairs, and bookshelves. An empty office.

He stepped back to the door, and then had an idea. "Althea?" he asked the empty room. He listened, to the count of twenty, for any sound at all. There was no sound.

Rooms 001 through 004 all seemed to be offices. Some of the bookcases had books lined up in them. None of the rooms had Althea in them. Neither was she in any of the stalls of room 005, a bathroom.

Room 006 was at the corner, and his flashlight showed a huge square thing that made him jump. Not because he was afraid, but because he was expecting a desk and chairs. He went up to it, silently on sneakered feet. A furnace. He examined all around it, anywhere a fifteen-year-old girl might be hidden. Nobody.

The numbers went back and forth, and so did Phineas, like a sentry pacing his guard area, except that at the end of each line of march he moved forward a little. Following the numbers, 007, cross a corridor, 008, 009, cross a corridor, 010, corridor, 011 against the parking lot wall again. All rooms empty of Althea, and some of them just empty rooms—he traversed the underground width of the library.

Rooms 012 and 013 were side by side, because 012 was in fact a broom closet. Cross a corridor to 014. Cross a corridor to bypass 015 since he didn't have a key that would let him into that room anyway. Rooms 016 and 017 were the opposite wall again, and both were small rooms, lined on two walls with filing cabinets. College records, he was willing to bet.

Phineas got the drill down: key in the door—018, 019—flashlight at floor level—020—then flashlight at shoulder level—021. Room 022 was hidden behind the staircase, narrow shelves stacked with paper towels and toilet paper, probably a hundred-year supply of toilet paper. Big whoopee. When the light was at shoulder level, he studied the walls carefully, in case there were closets—023, 024, 025.

He had to double back a corridor, turn right, then right at the next turning to find 026. Why couldn't they have numbered the rooms down the length of each corridor? It would have made his job easier.

The last step of the drill was calling her name. "Althea?" Each time he had to say it out loud it got harder to say it out loud. Rooms 027, 028, 029, 030. He said her name, and waited, to the count of twenty, his ears listening hard. The walls were thick, too thick for his voice to carry beyond the one room he was searching. If there had been any way for a mouse to get into this concrete rabbit warren, he'd have heard it move—so intently did he listen.

But he didn't hear anything, not the slightest movement, and certainly not a relieved and grateful voice saying his name, "Phineas?"

His flashlight found 032. Wrong. The beam went on to the corridor's end. Maybe he was at 032, maybe he'd miscounted, maybe—with everything the same—he'd gotten lost in the numbers. He turned right, walked up a few paces to another blank wall, and moved the flashlight until the light showed a number painted on the wall beside a door: 031.

"All *right*," Phineas said, relieved. His voice sounded normal. He was feeling almost normal, now, so accustomed was he to the drill. He was relieved to have found 031 so easily, because keeping track of the number he was on, and the count of twenty in each room, was about all his brain was up to, what with the worry, and the silence, and the solitude, and not finding her. He unlocked the door to 031, let the flashlight go around at floor level, and saw stacks of folding chairs folded up. He had no idea how long he'd been down here. Not only did he not know what direction he was moving in, with the darkness closing in behind him

169

constantly as he followed the light; he had also lost his sense of time.

Locking the door of 031 behind him, Phineas had a moment of panic. Had he done the complete drill? He thought so, but he wasn't sure. He was just going doggedly along, by now—however long it had been—no longer expecting to find her. It was like playing the last points of a lost set, just returning as best you could whatever your victorious opponent sent at you across the net, just not giving up.

He plodded back along his own path to 032. So he'd been wrong, even though he'd been sure. He wasn't really surprised—033, 034. He'd had no reason—035, 036. It was an idea. A guess. Just a feeling.

Phineas had half a mind to give up now, and stop wasting his time. Probably, if he found his way out again—he'd use the parking lot door to leave by—he'd get home to find out that Althea was there, probably tucked into her bed asleep, with the light on. But there was no reason—037, a corner room, some kind of office with phones this time, and a bulletin board; the Sports Department office as it turned out, a pile of lacrosse sticks against a wall rising out of a nest of helmets and pads; he didn't know they played lacrosse up here— There was no reason not to finish what he'd started. That way—he locked the door behind him—at least he could say for sure where she wasn't.

In case he got through here and went home and his father was there and they still didn't know where Althea was. Besides, he had to be almost through with the job. He traced his way back past 036 and 035, along the narrow corridor between 029 across from 034, and 030 across from 033, then turned left to find 039. Don't get sloppy, he reminded himself, turning the key in the lock. He had to be near the end—"Althea?" and a count of twenty slowly in his head, listening as hard as he could even though he didn't any longer expect to hear anything. It was when you were near the end of things, tennis matches, tests, that you tended to get sloppy—040—because the end was in sight. Because, with the end in sight, you started hurrying toward it, and that was when you made your careless errors. Like, trying a put-away shot that wasn't a sure thing. He locked the door of 041 behind him.

That was it. That was all the rooms.

Then where was she? What had happened to his sister?

When they found out, how bad was it going to be?

Phineas almost wished there were one hundred and forty-one rooms, with a lot still to search. As long as there was a room to look into, there was something to do. He didn't know why he'd been so stupidly sure of himself, thinking that he could think the same way whoever had done this would think. He went back along the corridor.

There was a jiggling in his brain. Like the feeling, as you walk home, that you didn't follow the directions on a test, that you'd screwed up.

Something was wrong.

Phineas turned out the flashlight. Of course something was wrong. What did he think, did he think he could fool himself? He felt—so bad, so sad and bad and scared. . . . This was about a million times worse than his feeling last spring, getting used to the idea of his mother going to live all the way across the country from them.

He made himself turn on the flashlight. He was going to have to go back home, and do nothing but wait again.

Thirty-eight, he thought.

Where had that number come from?

Had he done room 038?

He tried to think back, but he couldn't remember. But he would have noticed, wouldn't he have? He was keeping track. Was he sure he'd done every one? He wasn't even sure he'd done 009, or 021, just to pick a couple—or any of them, after 006. All he was sure of was that he had been methodical.

Room 038 stuck in his mind. Half of Phineas figured that he was just giving in to panic, and the other half thought that he was making up something to hope for. And it wasn't even that much to hope for, because even if he had skipped 038 there was no reason for Althea to be there, since she hadn't been in any other room.

But he went back along the corridors, turning left, turning right, to locate 037.

If only to shut himself up.

He checked to be sure 038 wasn't right next to 037, which it wasn't, then went back around the U-shaped corridor to find 039. Room 038 wasn't next to 039 either.

Maybe they'd skipped 038. Maybe it was an unlucky number, for some reason he didn't know, like sky-scrapers never had a thirteenth floor.

But wouldn't he know it if thirty-eight was a big un-lucky number?

You'd think he would, but he knew how much he didn't know. You couldn't live with two smart people and not figure out there was an awful lot you didn't know.

He opened the door to 039 again, and did the whole drill, which was easy because 039 was a little empty closet of a room. Not like 037, which was the Sports Department office, he remembered. It was closed for the summer, but he remembered that it was big enough for two desks, and a filing cabinet, and a pile of playing sticks up against the wall.

He trooped on back to 037. He wouldn't let himself run but he couldn't stop himself from thinking that he'd been in a lot of sports departments, between his own school and the schools where they'd gone to play against other teams in the elementary leagues. In all the sports departments he'd seen, there had been masses of equipment, a lot more than would fit into that office. There should be goals, and bats, and big baskets filled with soccer balls and basketballs. Not just a pile of playing sticks up against a wall.

He put the key into the lock, and reminded himself that there was a gym, the equipment he thought was missing from the room would be stored in the gym.

Yeah, but in that case the sticks shouldn't be piled against the office wall.

Besides, he told himself—and opened the door, and called out, "Althea?" No answer, so he called again, "Althea!" Besides, the gym was open over the summer, and all the sports departments he'd ever been near had been locked up tight at night. People stole equipment.

Phineas walked into the center of the room and pointed his flashlight at the pile of tall lacrosse sticks. The wall they leaned against was white, like all the other walls, but it wasn't rough cinder block. It was flat, like the doors.

He shifted the flashlight to his left hand, because he wanted his best arm for shoving stuff away, and he shoved, arm and shoulder, and the pile clattered onto the floor. The key shook in his hand. The door opened into darkness and he almost didn't dare shine the flashlight to look inside.

Lumps and shapes, just as he'd thought, equipment.

He heard something moving.

"Althea?" he whispered.

No answer, just thumpings, muffled thumpings.

It was her eyes he saw first, wide open, her eyebrows like dark inked lines. Then her face, her hair a frizzy mess around it. A broad strip of tape covered her mouth. She moved like a beached fish, with little flipping motions.

Even though he'd dropped the flashlight, there was still enough light to see by. Phineas knelt down beside the pile of football pads she lay on, to tear the tape off of her face.

"Ow! That hurts!" Althea cried, and then she leaned her head against his arm and burst into tears. "It *hurt*."

"It's okay," Phineas said, "everything's okay." He cradled her head for a minute, feeling just like his father when Mom collapsed into tears with whatever pressure had blown her sky high. "We can handle it," he said, over her sobs, just like Dad always said.

Althea nodded her head and sniffled. Phineas was sniffling with her, but he didn't much care. Then they were both laughing, wet teary laughs.

"I'm tied up." Althea rolled away, to show him.

And then Phineas did get angry. Anger was like a fire that dried his tears without any help from his hands or shirt, and cleared the sniffles out of his nose. She'd been tied like somebody in a prison camp, her wrists together behind her, her ankles tied together, and then the rope brought up to be tied to her wrists.

"I'm stiff. I hurt." She was getting teary again. "I wet my pants."

"So I smell," Phineas said, and couldn't figure out why that made her giggle. He was busy with the knots of the rope. He had to get the flashlight, but once he could see it wasn't hard to untie them. They weren't hard knots, not with both your hands free and a light to see by. They were just hard in the dark, with no way to move your hands. He'd never been so angry in his life. "Stretch out slow," he told his sister. He rubbed at her wrists with his hand while she was rubbing at her knees. "Do you think you can stand up?"

"You sound funny, Fin," Althea said.

"I'm okay," he told her, finding his jaw so stiff it was hard to move it.

"I'm okay, you're okay," she said, and giggled again.

The fire inside Phineas flamed up again. Dumb jokes and giggling—somebody had locked Althea away here in the dark for hours. She was probably going to be permanently nuts, and he could kill—seriously kill—whoever did that to her. First, smash his face in, then kill him—or her, he didn't care—

"Can you get up?" he asked again.

She got up onto her knees. Phineas stood up and reached down a hand.

"Hurts," she said again, sounding surprised.

"I know, but if you work the muscles—"

"What muscles?" she giggled.

Phineas shone the flashlight right into her face. Tear stains, blotchy face, and swollen eyes—she shoved it away. "What are you doing?"

"Looking at you," he said through his tight jaw.

"I'm okay. I'm just a little hysterical." Standing up she was bent over, like Igor. He reached out to help her with both hands, and she hugged him. Hugged him tight. "But I have to go to the bathroom, Fin."

Phineas just happened to know that room number 005 was a bathroom. They hobbled out together, and he even remembered to lock the doors. Althea leaned on him.

"How did you find me?" she finally asked, as they went down the corridor.

"By looking in every room," he answered.

"Persistence," she announced, sounding like herself.

"What hap—?" he started to ask, but she said, "First I really have to go to the bathroom, I can't even think—"

She could barely walk, either. Although, with every ten steps she walked better.

Phineas waited in the darkness outside of 005. Althea took the flashlight in with her, and he wasn't about to quarrel with her about that. He didn't even hear the toilet flush, the walls were so thick. She wouldn't have heard him call her name the first time into the Sports Department office. If he hadn't been keeping tabs on the numbers, he thought—

The door opened, and light emerged.

"It was Ken," Phineas announced, although he had no idea how he knew so surely who it was.

"I *told* you," Althea said, as if she had. Phineas figured she was in shock. He'd seen shock on TV. She didn't remember that she hadn't told anyone anything, that she'd just disappeared.

"Let's go home," he said.

❊ 18 ❊

By the time they'd come to the road, follow-ing the beam of light Phineas cast before them, Althea had begun to move her legs more easily. She had stopped groaning little groans at every step. She'd stopped hanging off of Phineas, using his shoulder to keep her balance. He still held her left hand in his right hand, with her forearm braced against his own, but that was all the help she needed.

They hadn't talked at all. They'd concentrated on keeping Althea moving, getting the blood circulating through her muscles again, getting the muscles work-ing. Phineas didn't ask her questions. He had a pretty good idea how bad Althea was feeling.

Himself, he felt terrific, seriously terrific. Their little house had lights shining in every window, like a birth-day cake. Phineas felt like John Wayne, bringing back the raw recruit he'd snatched away from the enemy. He felt like Han Solo at the end of *Star Wars*, with every-body applauding.

Their father must have been waiting just inside the door, listening, because by the time they got up the three porch steps he was outside. Hope hovered on his face for an instant before relief took over. He grabbed Althea into his arms, then pushed her away to look at her, then grabbed her close again. "You don't know how glad I am to see you," he said, including Phineas first in his glance and then in an arm that reached out to grab Phineas and pull him close.

"I need a shower," Althea said, sounding like a little girl.

"Then go take one," her father advised.

"But I don't want—"

"We won't. Cross my heart and hope to die, and stick a million needles in my eye, there'll be no talking until you get down," Mr. Hall promised. "Or," he corrected himself with an eye on Phineas, "nothing you'll want to be in on. I have something to say to you, young man."

Phineas couldn't think why he should be in trouble.

Althea turned at the doorway to ask Phineas, "You too."

"Promise," Phineas promised. The skin around her mouth looked raw, where he'd ripped the tape off. He could feel himself getting angry again, the seesaw balance sinking into anger as glad relief floated up, getting lighter. He was more angry than glad, seeing his sister's face, and he didn't much care if he was in trouble.

Phineas followed his father into the house, into the kitchen, where Detective Arsenault sat hunched over a mug. He looked big, even sitting down. He looked tired. He looked relieved. "Both of them," he said. "Thank God."

Mr. Hall turned around to face Phineas. He wasn't much taller than his son, but he was a lot angrier. Phineas had his own anger, as shield and weapon. His father ought to be grateful. Hadn't Phineas brought Althea back safe? He watched while his father's mouth tried to find words to get out. He knew what he'd done and he wasn't going to be bullied into thinking he hadn't done something terrific.

"You didn't even leave a note," Mr. Hall said.

Phineas's mouth fell open, but before he could get out an explanation or apology, his father was speaking again.

"How could you? Just take off like that? And not leave any word? And just let me come home to an empty house? And—"

"I'm sorry," Phineas said. "I didn't think of that. I should have, Dad, and I won't make the mistake again." He meant it, every word, including the sorry. He knew what it was like to have someone just disappear, and to have no idea where someone was. "I'm really sorry, Dad."

"I was so worried—" But that was the end of it for Mr. Hall. "Okay," he said. "Okay. You're back. You're both back." He ran his fingers through his hair, and then yanked at it, as if he needed to make sure he was awake, as if he was so glad he needed to do something physical to show it. Like, yanking at his hair.

"Don't pull it out," Phineas said, and felt like laughing. "Okay if I get myself a glass of milk?"

"Get me a beer, for celebration," his father said. "And a glass too please. Lou, do you want a beer?"

"I'm on duty," the detective said.

When they were all sitting and waiting, with the sound of a shower running upstairs, Mr. Hall asked Phineas, "Where did you find her?"

"In the library. In the cellar. But didn't you promise her we wouldn't talk about it until she gets down?"

His father ignored him. "In the cellar? Where?"

"We never even thought of looking there," Detective Arsenault said.

"There's a kind of equipment storeroom, behind the Sports Department office. I almost missed it," Phineas told them. "She was tied up, and taped over the mouth."

179

"Maybe we would have gotten around to it, room by room," the detective said. He didn't sound too sure of that.

The water stopped gurgling down through the pipes.

"She might never have been found," Mr. Hall said.

Phineas shook his head. His father wasn't thinking clearly. "No, as soon as they needed any equip—"

Which wouldn't have been until the start of the school semester, seven weeks. Unless there was an early start for varsity fall sports, say, the middle of August, say four weeks. Phineas had the feeling that four weeks was long enough to die in. He had the feeling that without water—and with your mouth taped you wouldn't be getting any water—it was more like seven days.

Gently, his father took the glass out of his hand.

If Phineas hadn't promised Althea not to say anything, he'd have set them off after Ken right away. With their guns. If it was too late, because he waited, kept his word—

"Phineas?" Althea was back in the room, in her bathrobe. Except for the skin around her mouth, she looked like nothing had ever happened to her. "You didn't tell, did you?"

He shook his head. He watched Althea take the milk carton and sit down. She took his glass for herself. "I'm thirsty," she said, and drank off a glass. She poured herself another. "Do you want to tell them?"

Phineas shook his head.

"Excuse me, Althea," Detective Arsenault said, "but we need to be sure. You are all right, aren't you?"

Phineas didn't know why he had to ask.

Althea did. "You mean, was I raped, or anything?" Althea asked, and she shook her head. "No, this wasn't about sex, it was about ambition. Ken's much more interested in his career than sex, I bet."

180

"Ken?" their father said.

Phineas looked at Althea and felt himself smiling back at her. It felt good to surprise people.

"Ken Simard?" their father said.

"Where is he now?" Detective Arsenault asked.

"England," Phineas said. "He's gotten away."

"But why would Ken do that?" Mr. Hall asked.

"We'll have him brought back," the detective said, and stood up to leave the room. Phineas was glad he wasn't the one Detective Arsenault was after in that tone of voice.

"Why, Althea?" Mr. Hall asked.

"For the poem."

"The poem? What poem?" Mr. Hall pushed his half-empty glass of beer away. "This doesn't make sense."

"Do you remember when I said there were Greek letters on the mummy's feet?" Althea asked. "And Ken put me down, as if I was an idiot?"

They didn't remember.

"Well, I was right," Althea said. "It was Greek. A Sappho poem, and I should have known right away, because the letters were the beginning of her daughter's name—Kleis. Anybody who's heard of Sappho knows about Kleis. But Ken sounded so sure of himself, I let him tell me something I didn't think."

Detective Arsenault returned to the table, looking satisfied.

"It was Ken who broke into the library?" Mr. Hall asked. Althea nodded. "And stole the mummy?" Althea nodded. "Because there's a Sappho poem on the wrappings?"

"Or a fragment. I didn't get a chance to look at the photographs he took. He took pictures, before he smashed her feet."

"I don't get it," the detective said.

"Late mummies, like in the Roman era, were sometimes wrapped in strips taken from papyrus sheets that were being thrown out," Mr. Hall explained. "According to Althea, our mummy's feet had the text of a poem by Sappho, who was—"

"I took a good ancient history course once, I know who you mean."

"But why would he care so much about an old poem?" Phineas wondered. "It's not as if it could be in her own handwriting."

"Unless it was a previously undiscovered one. One of the lost poems that we only know existed because other classical writers refer to them."

"See, Fin," Althea explained, "if Ken could discover it, and translate it, his reputation would be made. Like, do you remember the man who said he'd discovered a Shakespearean sonnet? He made the front page of the *Times*."

"So then Ken would get his job at Harvard." Phineas thought Ken Simard was dumb, dumb and disgusting. "I hope he gets sent to jail. I hope he gets sent to jail for life."

"Your mother!" Mr. Hall said, slamming his hand against his forehead. "You've got to call her, Althea, right now. She called earlier, said there was some woman here—?"

"Go call her, let her know you're both back safe. I had to tell her, Althea," Mr. Hall said.

"But don't talk any more about it until I get back," Althea said.

Phineas didn't know about the other two, but he felt like doing whatever Althea wanted, anything to make her happy. She didn't know how close she had come to dying, and he didn't see any reason to tell her. None of them said anything. They just listened to one side of a phone conversation.

Althea had barely finished dialing when she started talking. "Hi, Mom. Dad said I should call. No, I'm fine, really. I'll write you about it, okay? But I can't talk now, I just wanted you to know everything's okay, everybody's okay. I know you were, but it's over now. And I really do have to go, because there's a detective here and he needs the information. Okay, I'll call this evening, but now—I love you too."

Sitting down, Althea said, "I think I hurt her feelings. She wanted to talk."

"That's okay, she owes you some hurt feelings," Phineas said.

His father stared at him. Althea stared at him.

"Well, she *does*," Phineas said. Why were they staring at him?

Detective Arsenault had more questions for Althea. "How did you figure out that it was Professor Simard who was responsible?"

"When I thought about it, he was the only real choice. He was the only one who would have wanted to do all those things. Once I started to really think about it—Phineas, remember when we wondered if there was some backward reason? If the attempted break-in had been not to take anything, but to make Dad look bad?"

Phineas remembered.

"I started thinking like that," Althea said. "I started wondering if everything wasn't meant to deceive and misdirect us. The more I thought about that, and matched it up with what had actually happened—because what actually happened is the mummy's feet were destroyed. So the mummy's feet must have been what it was all about."

Detective Arsenault nodded his head as he listened. "I see that. I must admit, I never thought of Simard. Not seriously, that is, because I thought of all of you as possibilities, but—like you, Sam, he seemed just a professor, all wrapped up in academics, and not ambitious. Certainly not a criminal."

"That's because you were thinking about it like a criminal case," Althea said. "I was thinking about it like a scholar." She seemed to feel that that explained everything.

"Obviously, yours was the right way," the detective said.

"So I went to ask him about it," Althea said. Her voice slowed down, and she looked at her hands, the wrists coming out of the heavy terry cloth sleeves. "That was dumb. Because it *was* a criminal case. I thought it out, but I wasn't thinking. When I got there, he was home alone—his wife's in Boston on business. He was packing, and he told me to come on in. He looked different—I thought, because he'd shaved his beard. He looked sort of dangerous? Exciting? I was so dumb—I just blurted it out. And then—he's bigger than I am," she apologized, "and I don't know how to fight. He's not so strong, but if someone's smaller, and doesn't have any idea how to fight—anyway, he tied me up and put tape over my mouth so I couldn't yell. I couldn't do anything to stop him, I was helpless, useless. Then, he just finished packing, as if I wasn't there. It's a big house, Dad—and expensive. I guess his wife must make pots of money. They've got a water view, and there must be four bedrooms, the whole thing has been restored—like the Tunneys' house, remember that one? Almost a mansion, it was like that. He dumped me in the car. He told me, if I tried to show my head, or did

184

anything to attract attention, he'd kill me. I believed him. Because I was so scared."

Phineas looked at his father. His father looked at the detective. Detective Arsenault shook his head, just slightly.

But Althea was thinking, and worked it out. "I was right to believe him, wasn't I? That's what he was doing, wasn't it? He didn't mean me to be found. If he'd meant me to be found he'd have just dumped me in the hallway. Or in the collection room. Or the bathroom."

"So after you left the hospital you came back here, and worked it out." The detective's voice was low and calm, and calming. "Then you went over to his house to accuse him. At about what time was this?"

"Afternoon, early—I'm not sure. I can't believe I actually did that. Something so stupid."

"You should have left a note," Mr. Hall said.

"But I did. I left Phineas a message. Telling him who I thought was guilty."

"You did not," Phineas said.

"I did too."

"I never saw it. Where'd you leave it?"

"On my desk."

"All that was on your desk was some dumb doodling."

"That wasn't dumb doodling. It was in code. I shone my light onto it, Fin, so you couldn't miss it."

"Well, I missed it. Not the paper, just the message. Maybe there wasn't any reason to put it in code?" Phineas knew he sounded sarcastic.

"Anybody else would have figured it out. It didn't make any sense unless it was in code. Anybody except you would have known what it was."

"Oh, yeah? O'Meara didn't."

"O'Meara?" Mr. Hall interrupted their quarrel.

"She came by because she thought I might like the company, which I think was pretty nice of her. After she heard about Althea, on the police radio. I told you, she's the one that answered Mom's call."

"Hey, I think it's nice of her too," Mr. Hall said. "I'm not criticizing her. I'm just figuring things out. No wonder your mother called back."

Althea was not to be distracted. "Where's the paper now, Phineas? Go get it. You'll see. Jerk."

Phineas brought it in from the phone table. He studied it. So If Mom Asks Request Divorce. Okay, he saw it. "It only makes sense if you already know what it means," he said, and passed the paper to his father. "Kill every noodle," he muttered. "I mean, that's so complicated, Althea. It's too complicated to communicate."

"But it worked," she said. "If it didn't work, how did you know it was Ken?"

Phineas had no idea. "Just the same way I knew you were in the library, the way I know what time it is." He wasn't quarreling any longer. He didn't care much about understanding how, as long as things turned out all right. "Dad," he remembered. "I broke a window in the library, when I broke in. And I took keys from Mrs. Batchelor's desk." He pulled them out of his pocket and put them on the table, a show-and-tell. "I'll call in the morning, to tell her. It's not your fault, and I'll pay for it, I'll make sure she doesn't blame you."

"She can blame me as much as she wants to," his father said. "I don't even care much if I get fired. Just as long as you two are safe."

The detective pushed back his chair and got up. "That's all for now, I think. You must be exhausted, all of you."

Phineas discovered that he was. Fear and anger had

flowed out of him, and he was as tired as if he'd just played a four-set match.

"I know I'm exhausted and I've just been doing my job, plus some vicarious anxiety. Sam, can the three of you come to the station at—say three-thirty this afternoon? We should have him back by then."

"Sure."

"Don't get up, I'll let myself out."

"How will you get back?" Phineas asked.

"I left my car out of sight, behind the first house in the row," Detective Arsenault said. "I didn't want it to be seen, in case . . ." He didn't finish the sentence.

They didn't even bother rinsing off the dirty dishes. It was all Phineas could do to make himself put the milk back in the refrigerator before he went upstairs and fell onto his bed.

The house was dark, downstairs and upstairs. Phineas sat up, alarmed and awake. "Althea?" he called. The little house had its bedrooms so close around the hallway that they could all hear one another without raising their voices. None of them had their doors closed.

"What's the matter, Fin?"

"Are you all right?"

"Of course."

"But your light," he reminded her.

"I thought—" Her voice came out of the darkness.

"The light doesn't bother me," their father said, another voice floating on dark air.

"I know, but—I want to try it. I think, there's a difference between being scared and not knowing how you'll do, and being scared but knowing you'll do okay. I can always turn the light on, later."

"Yeah, well, if you do, close your door, okay? It

187

might not bother Dad, but it bothers me." Phineas would have been happy to continue the argument all night, but he was too tired to figure out how to do that.

✠ 19 ✠

"BUT WHY DID KEN STOP BY HERE, ON HIS WAY TO the airport?" Phineas asked. He swished the last bite of pancake around in the pool of maple syrup on his plate and popped it into his mouth. He *loved* maple syrup. If he'd been alone, he'd have leaned his face over to lick what was left on the plate.

"With your mouth closed, please," Althea said, for about the sixteenth time. Phineas closed his mouth and chewed on. "You're revolting," she said, just as he'd known she would.

"A few more?" Mr. Hall asked. Phineas nodded his head. Pancakes for lunch—but could it be lunch if it was the first meal you ate in a day?

"Anyway, why did he?" Phineas asked again. "The rest of it makes sense, trying to convince us that the crown was what the thief was after, and then calling up so the mummy would be returned safely. Even destroying her feet makes sense. But what's the sense in stopping by our house, when he—?"

Mr. Hall stood by the stove, watching over the pancakes on the griddle. They'd been up for a couple of hours, just talking about Ken, and what had happened, making sense out of all the pieces now that they knew how to fit them together.

"To gloat?" Althea suggested.

"That's a depressing thought," Mr. Hall said. He

slipped a stack of four pancakes onto Phineas's plate. "No more, the cook is retiring."

Phineas set to work buttering. "I don't think it was gloating. If it was me, if I'd been him—I think I'd have wanted to make sure we weren't suspicious of me. We weren't suspicious, were we, Dad?"

"Not a bit. Trusting babes, that's what we were."

"But what would he have done if you had been suspicious?" Althea asked.

Phineas poured syrup over the pancakes. He wasn't hungry, but they tasted so good he didn't want to stop eating. "What I'd have done in that case is gone back and turned you loose. That way, there was only the question of breaking and entering, and the damage to the mummy. That all could have been"—he took a bite, chewed, remembering to keep his mouth closed, and swallowed—"like, a plea of temporary insanity. A lighter sentence, or maybe even everything could have been hushed up."

"And if you weren't suspicious?" Althea asked. "Which you weren't."

"Then I'd have figured that I would get away with it," Phineas explained. "And felt pretty smart."

"But Fin, how could he think that when he still had to explain about the poem. Or the fragment, or whatever it is. People would ask where it came from, otherwise it could be a fake. How was he going to explain that?"

Phineas had no idea what Ken had in mind. "If it was me, I'd have hoped I'd figure out something, when I needed to. Ken looked like he thought he could do anything, didn't he, Dad? You didn't see him, Althea, he looked like he'd just tricked everyone into electing him president of the world. So he must have thought he
190

could get together a good enough story. As long as you didn't turn up to expose him.''

Phineas heard his own voice go stiff at the last sentence. So, apparently, did his father, because Mr. Hall's next question was, "You're not thinking of a career in crime, are you, Phineas? You seem to be revealing an aptitude for it, in the last twenty-four hours.''

Phineas grinned. It was a sort of compliment. Besides, they were all three sitting around their kitchen table, all freshly showered and ready to go together down to the police station, all well fed, and they'd been talking together about something they were all three interested in. Everything felt fine, everything was okay.

"What I have trouble understanding is how he thought he could get away with it," Mr. Hall said.

"I can't understand what he wanted to do it for, in the first place," Phineas said. "Except," he added, before anyone else had a chance to say anything, "he's a bad person.''

"Doesn't that depend what you think bad or good is?" his father asked. "If you define good as what benefits you—"

"Come off it, Dad," Phineas said. "Nothing that lets you tie somebody up, and gag them so they can't yell for help, and leave her where you hope she can't be found, can be good.''

"Not found until I was dead," Althea corrected, quietly.

Phineas hadn't wanted to actually say that.

"Listen, kids, I agree with you. I think you're absolutely right, Phineas. I'm just taking it from another angle, just thinking. In a way, it's survival of the fittest. The fittest survive, so if you survive you know you're fittest, so you do anything you can to survive.''

"That depends on what fittest means," Phineas ar-

191

gued. "I know about Darwin, but fittest is different for human beings. At least, in terms of what they ought to do."

"We hope so," his father said.

"My trouble is," Althea said, "that I can sympathize with him. No, I really can. I wouldn't do it, myself—I couldn't, at least I hope I couldn't, I can't imagine that I could, but—if Ken was the one to discover a Sappho poem, he'd be famous. His career would be made. Harvard might even call him up and offer him a job. You didn't see his house, Fin—it was expensive, and the kitchen had everything in it, huge stove and microwave, a little TV built into the wall, processor and blender, everything expensive, and—he must have felt like nothing next to his wife."

Phineas wasn't sure about either one of them. There was his father turning it into some philosophical question, and his sister looking at it as if it was part of the equal rights problem. As far as he was concerned, it was a bad thing to do and he was glad Ken had been caught. "I hope he rots in jail," Phineas said.

"Oh, so do I," his father agreed.

"Me too," Althea said.

"Then why are you justifying him?" Phineas asked.

"I'm not," Mr. Hall said, surprised. "There's no justification for what he did to Althea."

"Or the mummy," Althea added.

"Change of subject," Mr. Hall announced. "When we talk to your mother tonight, I want you two to go gently with her. One of the things she knew, without knowing how it would feel, is that we'd be able to get along fine without her."

"We almost didn't," Phineas pointed out.

"Yes, well, be sure she knows you think that," his

192

father said. "Are you two ready? Put your plate in the sink, Fin, and we'll go pick up O'Meara. Your date."

"She's not my date," Phineas said. "She was just hinting so badly, and she was here last night trying to help, and—it's not a date. Or," he turned the tables on his father, "if she's anyone's date it has to be yours, because you're the right age."

"I'm much too old for her," his father protested.

Phineas and Althea exchanged a look.

"And I'm not eligible," he said. "I'm *married*," he reminded them.

"There is that," Althea agreed, with mock solemnity.

20

AT THE POLICE STATION, THE HALLS WERE TAKEN into a room with glass walls and a glass door; in the center of the room was a long table. They sat around one end of the table, Althea between her father and Phineas, and O'Meara at Phineas's other side. "Wait here," they'd been told.

O'Meara took her pad and pen out of her big purse. She took a breath. "I didn't know that was your wife," she said. "If I had, I'd have said more, but how could I know? She could have been anyone. I don't know anything about your private life—well, not much anyway, I did know she lives in Oregon. Your wife. You aren't angry, are you? I can see why you might be and I do apologize. I can see she might have misunderstood. What I was doing at your house at that hour. I can see that I should have told her more. But do you mind if she's a little jealous? Or, wasn't she jealous? I don't want to assume anything, but she obviously misunderstood—and anyway, I don't think a woman should have children unless she's planning to stick around to take care of them as long as they need her. Although," she said, turning to Phineas and Althea, "I guess you didn't need her. Did you. I guess you did take care of yourselves. Wrong again, O'Meara," she said, and laughed a short laugh. "And to think that Dr. Simard is really a crook. And to think that I have the exclusive."

"You have it as long as you sit quiet," Mr. Hall said to her.

O'Meara nodded her head and pressed her lips together. She held her pen poised over the notebook. Her eyes shone.

Detective Arsenault came into the room, but he didn't greet them like a friend. He didn't sit with them, either. He sat at the center of one side of the table. Phineas decided that the detective had the kind of face, with bags under the eyes, that always looked tired, whether he was or not. "They're bringing him in now," the detective said.

Suddenly, Phineas wanted to go home. It was one thing to talk about Ken in the abstract, about what he'd done and why; it was another to think about having Ken actually there, facing them. Phineas squirmed in his chair. Althea sat quietly beside him.

Ken came through the door angry. He wore the same suit he'd worn the day before, only it was rumpled. Mr. Fletcher was right behind him, and one look at the stern lawyer, with his three-piece suit and his briefcase, made Phineas uneasy. If Mr. Fletcher was defending Ken . . . Phineas had the sudden uneasy sense that things might not be as simple as he'd thought.

Ken sat down at the opposite end of the table, with Mr. Fletcher next to him. It was like boxers in a ring, with the detective as referee, but Phineas wasn't sure who it was who was supposed to fight with Ken. As soon as he had sat down, Ken had something to say.

"What's this all about, Sam?" he demanded. "I'm glad to see that you decided to turn up, Althea. You had us all worried. But what's she doing here?" he asked, pointing at O'Meara. "Since when is the press present at what I take is a routine questioning?"

He turned, as if he expected Mr. Fletcher to say

something, but the man was taking a long yellow legal pad out of his briefcase, uncapping a thick black fountain pen. Mr. Fletcher didn't say anything.

Nobody said anything.

"Forgive me for being so dense," Ken said sarcastically. "You have to remember that I've crossed the Atlantic twice, in twenty-four hours. And not, mind you, on the Concorde."

Nobody said anything.

"Have it your way." Ken leaned back in his chair. He didn't look worried. He looked like someone who was about to play the winning card.

It made Phineas nervous. It wasn't the way the guilty person was supposed to look.

Detective Arsenault cleared his throat. "There is a charge of kidnapping."

"Who is it that I'm supposed to have kidnapped?" Ken asked. Then he looked at Althea. "Oh, Althea," he said, sounding as if she was a favorite student he'd just caught cheating on a test.

Althea studied her hands and didn't say anything.

"With what purpose am I supposed to have kidnapped her? I hope she isn't crying rape. I know she's attractive—"

Althea's head jerked up.

"—and intelligent, which can't help but appeal to me—"

Althea's cheeks were pink.

"—but she's just a girl. I'm a grown man, I wouldn't ever think of a schoolgirl as a—an object of passion."

He spoke with conviction and sincerity. Even Phineas believed him. But rape wasn't the question. Ken had taken the conversation and turned it into an accusation of something he was innocent of. In another minute, Ken would walk out, walk away, get away with it.

"You tried to murder her," Phineas said, since nobody else seemed about to say anything. He spat the words out of his mouth as if they were pieces of liver that he'd somehow bitten into. "Nobody would have gone into that storeroom for weeks, and you know that. You knew it."

"Is that what she said I did?" Ken asked. "Oh, dear. Oh, dear, Althea. I'm afraid I'm going to have to tell the truth about what happened. I didn't intend to, but now I have to. The truth is—I wasn't going to say anything to you, Sam, I was going to spare you this—that Althea came to my house. She came on to me, Detective, isn't that the phrase? Propositioned me. Of course, I told her no. She took it badly. I don't know where she went after that, or what happened to her, although I gather it was unfortunate. I am sorry, Althea," he said. "I never meant to tell anyone about the shameful scene."

"You're lying!" Althea cried. "He is, Dad. I did go to his house—and I told him what I knew—and he asked did I want a cup of tea—and did I want to see the darkroom—and he didn't deny anything. I don't even like him, why would I want to—" Her voice choked up. "Then he twisted my arm—and tied me up—and I didn't even know how to fight."

"Why should *I* lie?" Ken asked.

"Because of the poem!" Althea said. "Because you wanted to be the one to find the Sappho poem!"

Ken raised his eyebrows and looked at Detective Arsenault, as if he was too confused to make any sense out of all this. "I'm afraid I have no idea . . . ," he said, holding his hands out in a helpless gesture.

"Well," the detective answered, "we're searching your luggage, so there should be proof one way or another."

"And you think you'll find a three thousand-year-old manuscript there? I do hope that if that's what you think, you'll handle my things delicately."

"It was on the mummy wrappings!" Althea was practically shrieking. "And you know perfectly well it was! On the feet! Where you told me there weren't any Greek letters!"

"Ah," Ken said, super calm, super patient, hatefully grown up. "Now I begin to understand. So I'm supposed to have unwrapped the feet—and done what? Tucked the scraps into a plastic bag, to reassemble like a jigsaw puzzle? Give me a break, Althea. Nobody likes to be shown wrong about things, but this is carrying a grudge too far, isn't it? I can understand your desire to make yourself important, and I do feel sorry for you. I do understand the stress you're under, since your mother left home, left your father, left you—"

O'Meara put a hand onto Phineas's arm. He didn't know if that was supposed to soothe him or to make sure he didn't climb up to crawl down the table before anyone could stop him and slam his fist into Ken's lying mouth. But he didn't try to shake her hand off. He was pretty sure his father wouldn't let Ken get away with it, and he was pretty sure his father knew what was going on. His father sat quiet, thoughtful. Phineas tried to relax in his chair.

A patrolman in a blue uniform, but without the hat, knocked on the door. He came in, put a file folder down in front of Detective Arsenault, and left without saying anything. The detective opened the folder and took out two eight-by-ten black-and-white photographs.

Phineas strained to see. It looked like pictures of maggots, squirming in a pile, or a pile of bandages with dirt marks on them.

The detective passed the photographs to Mr. Fletcher,

who looked at them and passed them to Ken. Ken didn't even bother to look at them. He smiled, with white teeth and bright blue eyes. "Am I to assume that all of you know the difference between glyphs and Greek?"

The detective leaned forward. He didn't lean on his elbows, he just leaned his head forward, like a bear on its hind legs taking a closer look at a barking dog. "Don't assume anything about what I do or don't know, Dr. Simard. I'm sure Mr. Hall, and Althea too, can tell us if this is Greek."

"Of course it is," Mr. Fletcher said impatiently. He faced Ken. "Is there an explanation for this, young man?"

Ken looked at the pictures. "Oh, you mean these? I'd entirely forgotten them. Is this what all the brouhaha is about? If I'd known that, I'd have explained at Heathrow and saved myself a lot of time, and inconvenience too. You might have asked me there, instead of dragging me back, Detective."

Detective Arsenault didn't say anything.

"I had these in my attaché case," Ken said.

"We know," the detective said.

"Or you could have asked Sam. Sam knew I had them. He told me I could take the photographs."

Phineas saw his father out of the corner of his eye, his face growing red, and his eyes bulging a little. For a second, Phineas thought his father was going to blow up. But instead, Mr. Hall started to laugh. When he could speak, he said, "Outrageous. It's an outright lie. How can you hope to get away with this, Ken?"

Ken looked angry, and flustered too. "Because it's true. You knew I was taking pictures. I asked permission and you gave it. What are you trying to do to me, Sam?"

"But they're not feet," Mr. Hall pointed out. "Those

199

are photographs of the wrappings. These pictures show the wrappings after they've been taken off the mummy's feet.''

"Lies," Ken said, his voice rounding like a bell. "All lies. I don't know what you're after, Sam, but if you think they're going to believe a newcomer over the word of someone they've known for years—It's your word against mine, and I think I've earned the right to be trusted. Whereas you—who knows anything about you? Except that nothing like this ever happened at the college until you arrived. I have my reputation to speak for me." Ken's voice rang out.

"But Dr. Simard," O'Meara said, looking up from the pad she was writing on. "You're a liar. You're famous for it. Everyone knows. You do it whenever anyone stands up to you in an argument. Why do you think you only have lecture courses? The students complained because you lie like a rug when you're backed into a corner. You can ask anyone," she said to Detective Arsenault. "He's the Rugman, that's what we called him.''

Phineas almost laughed out loud—and then he thought he could kick himself. Hard. He could have known that all along. He'd known all along about Ken.

Ken stared at O'Meara for a minute and then deflated like a balloon. He looked at the detective. "You're going to take their word over mine? It's only their word.''

"I'm inclined to," Detective Arsenault answered. "But I suspect that if we look, we'll find proof. These pictures. The kind of tape that was used on Althea's mouth, the rope, a search of your darkroom—''

Ken hunched in his chair, glaring at all of them. Mr. Hall had his arm around Althea, who had covered her eyes with her hand.

"How could you do that to Althea?" Phineas demanded.

"She gave me no choice. The Sappho poem would make my career," Ken told him.

"It's just an old poem," Phineas said. He wished there was some way to tell Ken how—some words that, when he said them, Ken would just crumple up, destroyed.

"No, Phineas," Ken corrected him. "It's a treasure. A treasure for all the ages."

Althea took her hand down and moved back from her father's arm. "So was the mummy."

"It wasn't even a first-rank mummy. Fourth-rank, maybe, and we all know that. She was just some pretty girl of the Roman era, with terrific eyes—"

"How could you risk killing someone," Phineas demanded. "And she might have died." He saw the expression in Ken's eyes, which was anger, as if Ken was angry because he'd failed. They weren't even on the same planet, he and Ken. "Over a poem? Over words?"

"Art, Phineas. Art supersedes the individual."

"For your career," Phineas said.

"I'm a scholar. I could do first-class work in the right circumstances."

"You're a shithead," Althea announced. Nobody blinked at her language. "And a liar. And not even a real scholar." She sounded calm now, sure, like herself again. "A real scholar would never have destroyed the text. Or damaged the mummy."

"Who has proved that I did?" Ken asked. He turned to Mr. Fletcher. "You're my lawyer, do something."

Mr. Fletcher shook his head. "I told you, I am here at your request but my first loyalty is to the family. I'm the Vandemark lawyer. I warned you, young man, that if you were guilty, you didn't have to answer any ques-

201

tions. You told me you weren't afraid of questions. I warned you that if you were guilty, you'd be wise to confess. I expect that whatever criminal lawyer you find will give you the same advice."

"Well," Ken said. He studied his clenched-together hands. "Thanks a lot, Sam. You've scotched my career and I hope you're pleased. In case you care, you've also scotched my marriage. If she didn't like a nonentity for a husband, imagine how she'll feel about a jailbird. It's enough to make you laugh, isn't it?"

Phineas didn't feel a bit like laughing. He almost liked it better when Ken was lying. All he wanted now was for it to be over. And that, as if someone were reading Phineas's mind, was just what happened next. It happened rather quickly, just like on television shows, with the warning, and the policeman coming in to take Ken out of the room, into another part of the station. The only difference was, Detective Arsenault never said, "Book him."

It wasn't ten minutes later that they stood outside, in clear sunny air, watching Mr. Fletcher walk away. O'Meara was still with them.

"That wasn't fun," Mr. Hall said. "Does anyone else feel like a treat?"

"I should get to work," O'Meara said, but she didn't move away.

"Do we drive or walk?" Mr. Hall asked. He was trying to lighten the mood, Phineas could tell.

"Drive," Phineas said, trying to help.

"Walk," Althea said.

"Can we get ice cream?" Phineas asked.

"I want pastries," Althea said.

"O'Meara?" Mr. Hall asked. She shrugged; she didn't care which. "Then let's take the car and go down to the shore, and have ourselves a lobster dinner. We

202

have to be back in time to call your mother, but—how about it, O'Meara, do you like lobster?''

"Yes, but—"

"You can stay up all night writing your story. You're young, staying up all night won't slow you down. I haven't had a chance yet to thank you for coming to keep Phineas company last night," he said. "Or," he added, grinning, "for talking with my wife."

"About that," O'Meara said. "I already told you. I can explain."

✽ 21 ✽

ALL SATURDAY MORNING THE PHONE RANG, BECAUSE various members of the college community wanted to talk to Mr. Hall, for various reasons. Mrs. Batchelor, for example, wanted him to tell Phineas that she didn't blame him for breaking into the library and stealing her keys—she thought he was resourceful. Phineas wasn't sure he believed any of it, but he was relieved that that was what she said. President Blight wanted all three of them to come to a dinner, the next night. Other people just wanted to find out from an insider's view what had gone on, what Ken had really done. They wanted to know more than what was in the newspaper.

VANDEMARK PROFESSOR CHARGED IN KIDNAPPING, that was one of the headlines. PROF'S DAUGHTER DISCOVERS TREASURE, that was another, with a photograph of Althea beneath it. MUMMY'S CURSE GOES TO COLLEGE: That one Phineas would have bet money O'Meara had written herself.

Anybody who could think up any excuse to do so, called. Between calls, the three Halls exchanged information and opinions, trying to remember just what they were thinking and doing when one thing or another had happened. By afternoon, the calls had subsided and the Halls were talked out, but they couldn't seem to settle down.

Phineas knew what it was. It was the Letdown. He always felt it after a big game or a tennis match, win or lose, and he'd learned to anticipate the curiously flat feeling, the feeling that something should be going on and wasn't. But his father and sister didn't have any experience of it, so it was Phineas who suggested that they go to the movies Saturday night.

He hadn't expected the recognition Althea got, the way strangers stared at her as they stood in line to see *Batman*. Althea didn't mind it a bit. The movie was just what he had expected, a distraction. Phineas thought it was funny, and he thought the special effects were terrific. Seriously terrific. Especially the car. The other two didn't like the movie one bit. His father kept carrying on about the malice of the Joker—painting over great art, or gassing a crowd of people under a shower of money. "Worse than anarchy, somehow," he said. "It's like, malice in a vacuum."

"It's only a movie, Dad," Phineas reassured his father. "It's a joke." But his father didn't see any humor in it, and Althea was practically frothing at the mouth. "She's supposed to be a news photographer, who has reported on war, and all she does is scream. Because she's in the woman's role."

"It's only a movie," Phineas argued, but they weren't listening to him. He guessed that if he wanted to see it again, and he did, he was going to have to find someone else to go with. He wondered if Casey would be interested.

At least his plan had succeeded. They weren't even thinking about the mummy, or Ken, or Sappho.

By Sunday they were all settled down again. Phineas and his father were in the kitchen after a late breakfast. A slow rain drizzled down outside the windows. Mr. Hall was clipping newspaper articles to send to his wife. Piled up on the table he had the Portland paper and two Boston papers, as well as scissors and a stapler. Phineas had rescued the comics and the sports section, but he had to lie on the floor to read, because his father had the whole table filled. Althea came in to run water into the kettle.

Phineas looked up at her, in her bathrobe, with her hair frizzing out and onto her shoulders. "What are you doing upstairs?" he asked.

"Working."

She took down a mug, spooned honey into it, and added a tea bag. "You know, Dad, if we're going out for dinner tonight, you have papers that have to be corrected, and the week's lessons to plan. This afternoon."

Mr. Hall looked up, scissors in his hand. "I'm almost through with this. Your mother will enjoy these. I think she's a little jealous."

"Of course she is," Phineas said. "She's missing all the fun and excitement."

"She also feels guilty for not being here," his father pointed out.

Phineas knew that. He didn't need to be told.

"You know, I don't think she had any idea how much work her job was going to be," Althea said. "She told me she works twelve to fourteen hours a day, and six or seven days a week. I don't think she expected that."

"She likes to be busy," Phineas said. When they both turned to give him a Look, he added, "It's a good thing we're not living with her. We'd just be trouble. She'd really feel guilty then, if she was neglecting us and we were right there."

"Your mother's too intelligent not to have understood that the kind of fundamental changes women want to make won't be easy," Mr. Hall said.

"That's no reason not to make them," Althea said.

"I never said it was," he answered.

The water boiled and Althea poured it into her mug. They weren't talking about Ken at all, and Phineas was glad of that. He didn't want to think about Ken, and what Ken had done, and what was going to happen to him. They'd have to testify at a trial, unless Ken pleaded guilty, but until then they seemed to have agreed to forget about him. They would get through a trial if they had to, together. They didn't need to say that to one another.

The phone rang, *blatt-blatt*, but Althea was on her way back upstairs so she answered it. "It's for you, Fin," she called. "Casey."

Phineas went to the phone. "You made the *Times*," Casey said. "Did you see it?"

"We made the *Times*, Althea," Phineas called up to her feet.

She turned around and sat on the stairs.

"Do you want to come down for the day, or the night?" Casey asked.

"I can't. We have to have dinner with the president."

Casey hesitated to ask. "Bush?"

Phineas laughed out loud. "No, President Blight. Isn't your father going to be there? I thought it was like a celebration dinner, and your father would have to apologize to mine."

"He is going up for the dinner. But I don't think my father knows how to apologize."

"My dad's been practicing his modest smile," Phineas said.

"How about Tuesday, then," Casey asked. "I have sailing all day tomorrow, but Tuesday—"

"I'll ask," Phineas said.

"Althea could come along too if she wanted to, if she's bored, or lonely, or . . ." Casey's voice trailed off.

Phineas looked at his sister, and wondered. He frowned, watching her. You might find Althea seriously attractive, if you liked a face that looked like the person behind it had a lot of her own ideas and would fight about them if you crossed her.

"I'll ask," Phineas said. "I'll call you right back, is that okay?"

"Great," Casey said.

"Or if you'd rather, you could come up here and meet our famous mummy," Phineas offered.

"I'd like that too," Casey said. "George can do all the driving, so there's no problem with transportation."

"Nice to be rich," Phineas said, and right away he wished he hadn't. It was a pretty dumb thing to say to someone you didn't know at all.

But Casey was smiling, he could hear it. "I'm not complaining."

Phineas hung up laughing. "He wants me to come spend Tuesday," he reported to his sister. "He wants you to come too, if you'd like."

She shook her head.

"I think maybe he's got sort of a crush on you."

Althea's cheeks turned pink and she ignored that. "I'm going back to work."

"What's so important?" Phineas asked. "You could meet people."

"I'm trying to make a translation of that poem," she told him. "Detective Arsenault let me Xerox a copy of the photographs, and I want to try it on my own, before the scholars do it. I know I can't make a good one, I don't know enough about putting the words together, what order they probably go in, or the vocabulary, or the syntax, I know that, but—before I read the rest I want to try my own. I know you think I'm weird, Fin. Don't bother saying it."

208

"I don't think you're weird," he said. "And I wish you'd stop telling me what I think. It's pretty annoying, someone doing that."

"Sorry." Althea sounded like she meant it.

"It's okay," Phineas told her. He had a sudden idea and said, before he thought, "I don't like thinking about Ken either."

"I guess," she answered slowly, "we can't help it. I guess it's dangerous not to think about him. Because I don't think he feels all that differently than I do about this Sappho poem, but I'd never . . . Phineas, if I told you I was thinking I'd like to take a karate class, would you laugh at me?"

Phineas shook his head no. But he was biting the inside of his cheeks to keep from laughing at the idea of Althea doing karate.

"I couldn't fight back at all. I couldn't defend myself. I was as helpless as the mummy. And the mummy's dead. I asked you not to laugh," she said.

"I'm not," Phineas said, and it was true.

"So, will you take it with me?" Althea asked.

Then Phineas did laugh. "Sure," he said. "Why not?" He'd seen *The Karate Kid* lots of times, he knew how to do it. He bent his knees, brought his hands up flat to chest level. "Hi—yah!" he cried as he kicked his left leg out, stiff. "Hiii—yaaaah!" and he stepped down onto his left foot, chopping viciously with his right hand.

"Jerk," Althea said. "You saved my life, but you're still a jerk."

About the Author

Cynthia Voigt is the author of fifteen other novels, including Newbery Medal Winner *Dicey's Song* and Newbery Honor Book *A Solitary Blue*. *The Vandemark Mummy* is her second mystery. Her previous mystery, *The Callender Papers*, won the Edgar Allan Poe Award in 1984.

She was the recipient of the 1989 ALAN Award, given by the Assembly on Literature for Adolescents of the National Council of Teachers of English for her significant contribution to the field of adolescent literature.

Mrs. Voigt lives in Maine with her husband and two children.

Look for these books by

CYNTHIA VOIGT

in your local bookstore.